JINGLE BELLS AND DEADLY SMELLS

A Sandy Bay Cozy Mystery

By

Amber Crewes

D1527490

Amber Crewes

ISBN: 9781096872474
Imprint: Independently Published

Jingle Bells and Deadly Smells

Other books in the Sandy Bay Series

Apple Pie and Trouble

Brownies and Dark Shadows

Cookies and Buried Secrets

Doughnuts and Disaster

Éclairs and Lethal Layers

Finger Foods and Missing Legs

Gingerbread and Scary Endings

Jingle Bells and Deadly Smells

A

Sandy Bay

COZY MYSTERY

Book Ten

Amber Crewes

1

IT WAS GOING TO BE A WHITE CHRISTMAS in Sandy Bay, and Meghan Truman could hardly contain her excitement as the glittering white snowflakes tumbled from the sky. Meghan shivered as she adjusted the pink tartan scarf around her neck, thankful for its comfort as she stepped outside into the chilly evening. Meghan set off down the street toward Spark, a new boutique in town. She was ten minutes late for her shopping date with Jackie, her close friend, and Meghan trudged through the snow in her knee-length brown boots.

"Can you spare a dime, Miss?"

Meghan bit her bottom lip as a homeless man on the corner beckoned her toward him. She nervously ran a hand through her long, dark hair, shaking her head as she passed.

"I'm sorry," Meghan muttered as she looked down at her boots. "I don't have any cash."

Her heart sank as she walked away from the homeless man, and her cheeks burned with shame. She truly did not have any cash on her, but her chest tightened with guilt as she considered the man's plight. "Perhaps I could have given him my gloves," she thought to herself. "Or I could have dashed home and fetched some treats for him from the bakery."

She was the sole owner of Truly Sweet, a wildly successful bakery in Sandy Bay. She had opened the bakery after moving to Sandy Bay from Los Angeles less than a year ago, and now, after months of persistence and perseverance, Truly Sweet was one of the most popular bakeries in the Pacific Northwest. Meghan's orders had more than quadrupled in the last three months, and she was thankful for the help of Trudy, her assistant, and Pamela, the high-school girl she had hired to help with the heavy workload.

"I have so much stale bread and old pastries sitting in my pantry," she murmured, still distraught by her interaction with the homeless man. "It is so cold tonight, and he needs to eat. I will just have to be a few more minutes late to my shopping date."

Meghan turned around, treading back through the heavy snow. She unlocked the front door of the bakery, smiling as the familiar sound of the little silver bells attached to the door jingled merrily. She heard her little twin dogs barking upstairs in her apartment, but she ignored them, sprinting into the kitchen of the bakery and removing a bag of old pastries and breads from the closet.

"Perfect," Meghan said, satisfied as she filled a cloth sack with the food. "I can drop these off with that man, and hopefully, he will go to bed with a full belly tonight."

She raced out of the bakery and back onto the slippery streets. She nearly fell as her feet slipped beneath her, but she regained her composure and marched off toward the corner where she had encountered the homeless man.

"Oh no," Meghan sighed as she arrived to find the man had vanished. "He's gone. I was too late."

She hung her head, wishing she had had something to give the man when she first met him. "Maybe I'll see him again someday," Meghan considered as she rested the bag of food down on the side of street. "Maybe he'll come back. I'll leave this food here for now. I hope he finds it."

Jackie chastised Meghan as she entered the shop. "Where have you been? You are too late, girlfriend. This is the second time this week you've been late to a hang out."

Meghan's cheeks burned, and she sheepishly apologized to Jackie, explaining why she was late.

"Oh, Meghan," Jackie said kindly as she saw the tears in her dark eyes. "You were full of the holiday spirit. I'm proud of you. What a good person you are."

Meghan shrugged. "I just think everyone deserves a full belly and a warm bed, don't you?"

Jackie smiled. "Your heart is truly sweet, Meghan. Hey, speaking of Truly Sweet, are you doing the desserts for Jack's holiday party?"

Meghan grinned at the mention of Jack Irvin, her handsome detective boyfriend. "No," she explained to Jackie. "Chief Nunan reached out and asked me to do the desserts, but I decided to pass the chance up; I want to go to the party as a guest, and I think dealing with the desserts would be a lot of stress."

Jackie nodded. "That makes sense," she told Meghan. "Well, the Sandy Bay Police Department Christmas Party is always a huge event in town. Everyone dresses up, and there is mistletoe, and it's just magical."

Meghan smiled. "I need to find the perfect dress; do you think I would look nice in red velvet?"
Jackie squinted her eyes at Meghan, looking up and down at her curvy frame. "Yes," she finally replied. "I think with your dark hair and olive skin, you would glow in red velvet. Come on! Let's see what this shop has to offer."

"Ladies!"

Meghan and Jackie turned to find Kirsty Fisher beaming at them, her blonde bob sitting elegantly just above her shoulders, and a strand of tiny pearls wrapped around her thin neck. Kirsty was a dedicated philanthropist and organizer in the community; if there was an event or party, it was likely that Kirsty had planned and put on the event, and she was always looking for favors as she dreamed up new functions for the town.

"So good to see you girls," Kirsty cooed as she gave Meghan and Jackie air-kisses on both cheeks. "In fact, I was just thinking of you, Meghan. What are you doing next weekend?"

Meghan grimaced. "Why do you ask, Kirsty?"

Kirsty adjusted her red and green sweater set and smiled warmly. "I'm organizing a celebration of Christmas carols, and I would love if you could help me."

Meghan paused. She had intentionally slowed her schedule over the last week, and she was looking forward to some much-needed rest and recuperation after such a busy, eventful year in Sandy Bay.

"Kirsty," Meghan began. "I'm not really taking on new orders right now; I'm not even doing the desserts for Jack's holiday party. It's been a hectic year, and I am trying to give myself, along with Trudy and Pamela, some time to catch our breath."

Kirsty shook her head. "I don't want your treats," she informed her. "I need your voice. I am trying to recruit anyone and everyone to participate, and for a small donation, you can join in the fun."

Meghan raised an eyebrow. "I have a terrible voice," she told Kirsty. "It's horrendous; I was actually cut from my middle-school choir because I am tone-deaf."

Kirsty waved her hands dismissively. "You can just lip-sync, then. Jackie, I'm sure you can sing on pitch. Would you join us?"

Jackie wrinkled her nose. "My voice isn't good…"

Kirsty huffed in frustration. "This is for a good cause, girls," she informed Meghan and Jackie. "The donations are being given to the local homeless agency, and with the holidays just around the corner, it is important to think of others."

The image of the homeless man on the corner from earlier flashed through Meghan's mind, and she nodded emphatically. "Yes, you are right," she said to Kirsty. "We'll both be there."

Kirsty tossed her blonde hair behind her shoulder and smiled haughtily. "That's what I wanted to hear," she told both ladies. "Wonderful. Just bring something for the homeless folks who attend. You can even bring something store-bought, Meghan. Just make sure you have something for them, as well as your donation. Toodles, girls! See you at the Christmas carol."

Jackie rolled her eyes as Kirsty sashayed out of the boutique. "How did we just get roped into that?"

Meghan shrugged. "Kirsty is right," she told Jackie. "It's the season of love and giving. I can whip up a batch of cookies to take with me, and we'll both go. Besides, it's only for a few hours, and it's for a great cause. What could go wrong?

On the evening of the event, Jack picked Meghan up from the bakery. His blonde hair was smoothed down with gel, and Meghan thought he looked handsome in his green Christmas sweater.

"Thanks for going with me tonight," Meghan said to Jack as she leaned up on her tiptoes to kiss him softly on the lips.

"Of course," he replied. "It's a good cause, and I'm proud of you."

Meghan smiled. "It will be fun. It's always good to give back."

Jack and Meghan drove to the Sandy Bay Community Center, and as he helped Meghan out of the car, her eyes sparkled with joy. "Look at the decorations," she cried, pointing to a ten-foot high Christmas tree positioned outside of the main entry. "It's beautiful."

Jack playfully swatted Meghan on the arm. "Don't you know by now that Sandy Bay knows how to celebrate?"

Jack took Meghan's hand as they entered the massive main room. Meghan saw Kirsty assembling carolers onto bleachers, and she waved at Jackie from across the room. "I'm going to go get settled. Can you put my cookies on that dessert table over there?"

Jack nodded, taking the bag from Meghan's hands. "Of course. You go have fun!"

Meghan scurried over to where the singers were corralled, but as she began to ascend the stairs to her row on the bleachers, she heard a shout. Meghan turned to see four men shoving each other next to the dessert table.

"I want all of those cookies. You ate too much cake."

"Don't be selfish. My kids need some food too."

"This stupid party was the only way to get some good food, and I'm going to take what I want."

Meghan saw one of the men reach into the bag and take out her cookies. From his tattered clothes and greasy hair, she presumed he was homeless. She watched in horror as he threw her cookies onto the floor.

"I'll be right back," Meghan whispered to Jackie as she took off across the room. "Hey, sir? Sir? I only made enough so that each person could have two cookies."

The man scowled, but he nodded at Meghan. "Sorry. I was just excited."

Meghan felt a hard tap on her shoulder. She heard Jack's deep voice coming toward her. "Don't you touch her!"

Meghan's heart beat faster as she turned around. Jack ran to her side, but as she made eye contact with the man who touched her shoulder, she gasped.

"What do you think you are doing?" Jack demanded as he stepped between Meghan and the man. "Keep your hands off of my girlfriend."

The man chuckled, winking at Meghan. "Who do I think I am? Meghan, honey? Wanna tell 'em?"

Meghan's jaw-dropped. "Daddy," she whispered. "Daddy, I can't believe you are here.

2

"THIS IS YOUR FATHER?" Jack asked Meghan in a panicked voice.

Meghan nodded. "Jack, this is my father. Daddy, this is my boyfriend, Jack."

Jack reached out his right hand, and it shook as he extended it. "It's an honor to meet you, Mr. Truman," Jack breathed anxiously as Meghan's father peered down at him.

"Call me Henry," Meghan's father ordered.

"Henry," Jack repeated obediently. "It's a pleasure to meet you."

Jack was a tall man, but Henry Truman was even taller; Meghan's father towered over Jack, making Jack look like a little boy. Henry was also brawnier than Jack; Mr. Truman's muscles protruded from his expensive-looking shirt, and Meghan could not believe how intimidated Jack appeared beside her father.

"I'm so sorry to have stood in your way," Jack

apologized as Henry stared at his outstretched hand. "I didn't know…."

"Put your hand down," Henry commanded as he planted a paternal kiss on Meghan's forehead. "I'll shake your hand when I've been properly introduced by my daughter. Meggie, sugar, who is this fellow? Is this the boy you've been speaking to your Mama about when you phone us in Texas?"

Meghan nodded. "Yes," she admitted. "Daddy, this is Jack Irvin of the Sandy Bay Police Department. Jack, this is my father, Henry Truman, CEO and founder of The Truman Oil Company."

Henry winked at his daughter. "That was a proper introduction. Okay Jack, now I can shake your hand."

Henry grabbed Jack's hand and pumped it vigorously, and Meghan watched as her boyfriend's face turned beet-red. "Daddy, you're hurting him," she softly protested. "Where's Mama?"
Henry let go of Jack's hand, but he did not break eye contact with Meghan's boyfriend as he answered her question. "She's resting at our hotel," Henry said as he smiled down at his daughter, his own dark eyes sparkling. "She's very excited to see you; it was her idea to surprise you here in Sandy Bay during the holidays, and by the look on your face, I can tell that you had no idea we were coming up this way."

Meghan grinned at her father, and wrapped her arms around his neck. She breathed in the familiar, musky scent of *Brut*, his favorite cologne, and she laughed as she recalled the frightened look on Jack's face.

"Daddy, you pulled one on me. I can't believe you and Mama came up here."

Henry's face fell. "We feel terrible that we didn't visit you when you lived in Los Angeles," Henry told her quietly. "With so many children, and my business, it was just too much. Your Mama and I want to make it up to you now; we're staying for a whole week!"

Meghan clapped her hands in excitement. "Who is home watching the children?" she asked, thinking of her many younger siblings back in Texas.

Henry smiled coyly. "We hired a nanny," he informed her. "His name is Garrett, and he is quite helpful; he cooks, he cleans, and he makes sure all things run smoothly at home. Your Mama is an angel for electing to stay home with all of her children, and having another pair of hands has been so good for her nerves."

Meghan beamed and took her father's hands. "I'm just so happy the pair of you are here. Sandy Bay is adorable, and I cannot wait to show you the bakery."

Henry hugged his daughter. "I cannot wait to see what your hard work has resulted in," he whispered into her ear. "You've always been my good girl, Meghan. Your mother and I are so proud of you."

Jack stepped into the conversation. "Can I suggest dinner? We could all go out and get to know each other. My treat."

Henry shook his head. "Shhh, John, can't you see I'm

having a conversation with my daughter?"

Meghan giggled. "It's Jack, Daddy."

"Jack, John, same thing," Henry sighed. "Dinner is out of the question tonight; your mother is fast asleep in the hotel room, and I am about to drop dead of exhaustion myself. We will plan on being at your bakery bright and early, Meghan, for a grand tour. What do you say?"

Meghan blushed. "It's a small bakery, so it is not quite grand, but yes, please come!"

Jack cleared his throat. "It's a *great* bakery," he protested. "You should be proud."

Henry raised an eyebrow at Jack. "Let my daughter speak for herself. Anyway, we will see you tomorrow, Meghan. We love you."

Meghan's heart warmed as her father kissed her head, and she squeezed his hand. "Thank you for coming, Daddy. I'll see you tomorrow."

As Jack and Meghan drove home from the event, Meghan could see that Jack was flustered; his cheeks were red, his eyes were narrowed, and his hands were white as he gripped the steering wheel. Meghan knew that her father had not been particularly warm to Jack, but she was unfazed; Henry Truman was notorious for being cold and aloof with his daughters' boyfriends, and Meghan thought that their introduction had gone well.

"I think he really liked you," she assured him as he turned onto her street.

"Oh? What gave you that impression? When he wouldn't shake my hand at first, or when he corrected me for speaking up for you?" he responded angrily. "Why didn't you tell me they were in town? Some notice would have been nice, Meghan."

Meghan shifted awkwardly in her seat. "I didn't know they were coming," she insisted as she tucked a stray dark hair behind her ear. "You heard the conversation, babe. I had no idea. They never visited me when I lived in Los Angeles, so I never expected to see them here without even a word."

Jack sighed. "I know," he said softly. "I heard. I'm just annoyed with myself for not making a better impression on your father. You are important to me, Meghan. I love you. You are so special to me, and someday, who knows? Maybe your father and I will be family. I just want him to respect me as someone who cares deeply for his daughter and treats her well."

"He will," she pleaded. "Just give him some time. He will come around to you, Jack. I promise: by tomorrow, the two of you will be the best of friends!"

———————————————

"I don't like him," Henry whispered into Meghan's ear as they walked into Luciano's, Meghan and Jack's favorite Italian restaurant in Sandy Bay. "He just seems too nervous."

"He *is* nervous, Daddy," she told her father as the tuxedo-clad waiter guided the group to their table. "Just give him a break. I really like this one."

At nine that morning, Henry and his wife, Rebecca, had shown up at Truly Sweet. "Darling," Meghan's mother had cooed as she embraced her. "It is so nice to see you. Daddy told me you were so surprised."

"I was," Meghan affirmed as she brushed a small piece of lint from her freshly-ironed collared shirt. She had carefully chosen her outfit with her mother's fine, Southern taste in mind, and Meghan was proud of the ensemble she had selected. Her collared shirt was carefully tucked into a maroon and tan skirt, and a matching maroon sweater was carefully draped across her shoulders. A string of bulbous white pearls graced Meghan's collarbone, and the buttons on her shirt matched the tiny buttons on her brown leather boots.

"Are those your house clothes?" Rebecca asked her daughter, eyeing Meghan's outfit. "Surely you don't often wear those things around guests. Run upstairs and change, Sugar."

Meghan said nothing, but she turned on her heel and dashed upstairs to change. "My mother has never approved of the way I look, or the way I dress," she grumbled to her dogs who were resting peacefully on her bed. She wrestled with the buttons of her blouse. "With her little waist and long, glossy blonde hair, my mother has always looked like a doll. My sisters look just like her. I'm the only one in the family with dark hair, dark eyes, and curves. I just wish she would think about something else for a change instead of the way I look."

"Meghan? What is taking so long?" she heard her mother call as she threw a pale pink sweater over her head.

"Be right down," she replied, thinking back to how similar this encounter felt to her days in Texas as a teenager.

As Meghan descended the steps, she saw her parents admiring a display case filled with holiday-themed pastries. "Those were made fresh this morning," she announced. "I tried to incorporate all of the winter holidays with my designs."

"They are simply fabulous," Rebecca murmured as she gingerly picked up a cookie in the shape of a dreidel. "You are so creative, Meghan. I'm so happy you decided to give up on being an actress. Your creativity is better suited here in the bakery."

Meghan smiled. "Thanks," she said to her Mum. "I'm happy here, and my business is thriving; I've been written about in five magazines this year, and I'm excited to see what next year brings."

Henry patted his daughter on the head. "Your entrepreneurial spirit is impressive," he declared to her. "You've really made this a special thing. Your mother and I are so proud of you."

Before Meghan could thank her parents for their compliment, Jack burst into the bakery. "Hey, everyone," he said as he clumsily reached for Rebecca's hand. "You must be Meghan's mother. It's nice to meet you, Mrs. Truman."

Rebecca eyed Jack up and down. "It's Rebecca," she said dismissively. "You must be John."

Jack bit his lip, but Meghan shushed him before he could correct her mother. "It's Jack," she murmured. "Jack Irvin. He is a detective. Isn't that exciting?"

Rebecca said nothing, but walked to stand next to her husband, threading her arm through his.

"Meghan? The hotel we're staying at really serves great food but I'd like something different today. Is there somewhere you could recommend?"

Jack began to nod, his overexcitement making Meghan uncomfortable. "Luciano's!" he shouted. "It's our favorite Italian restaurant. Let's take them there, Meghan."

Meghan shook her head. "My mother doesn't like Italian. She doesn't eat carbs."

Henry waved his hand. "It's fine, Sugar," he told Meghan. "If Johnny here wants to take us out for Italian, then we'll go eat Italian. Let's see what kind of taste Johnny here has."

3

AS THE TRUMANS AND JACK WALKED
towards Luciano's, Meghan's heart crumbled as she
spotted a group of homeless people begging for
change. They looked exhausted, and Meghan felt
guilty as her parents shepherded her toward the
expensive Italian restaurant.

"Can I sing to you folks for a dollar?"

The group turned to see a middle-aged man in a
tattered trench coat smiling at them. He was wearing
a scraggly white beard and a Santa hat, and his
disheveled appearance, as well as the stench emitting
from his clothing, was impossible to ignore.   He had
an enormous pair of headphones atop his head, and he
bobbed and swayed to the soft strains of music that
came out of the speakers.

"Daddy, let's listen to him," Meghan pleaded as her
father tugged on her arm. "He wants to work for our
money. Let's give him a listen."

Henry shook his head. "It's not in good taste to
appease *those* kinds of people," he whispered to
Meghan as Mrs. Truman ducked inside the restaurant.

"You should know better than that."

"Meghan! Ciao, Bella."

Roberto Luciano, the Italian-born founder and owner of Luciano's, bustled outside. "Is this man bothering you? It's been bad for my business to have this group hanging out around here. Come, let me usher you inside. Dessert is on the house tonight."

Meghan smiled kindly at Roberto. "It's good to see you, Roberto. This is my father. He and my mother are visiting from Texas."

Roberto's face glowed. He leaned over and kissed Henry on both cheeks. "I can only say grazie to you for choosing Luciano's," Roberto cooed. "This is the best Italian restaurant in the Pacific Northwest, if I do say so myself, and Meghan and Jack come here often."

Meghan saw Jack shiver as a gust of ocean air stung his cheeks. "Come," Roberto said as he saw Jack's shoulders shake. "It's a cold night. Let's get you all inside and warm you up with some fettuccine. Again, my apologies for this...sight....outside of my restaurant."

Meghan waved apologetically at the group of homeless people, feeling guilty that she was about to go enjoy food and fun with her family when these folks were stuck in the cold.

"Don't think about them," Jack said, seeing the sad look on Meghan's face as they walked into the restaurant. "let's just enjoy our dinner, Meghan. There's nothing you can do to help them."

Meghan nodded and followed Jack inside of the restaurant. The dining room was painted in deep reds, smoldering oranges, and soft yellows, and Meghan felt as though she had been whisked away to Tuscany. Italian songs played softly on the radio, and the room was aglow with flickering candle light that made the large space feel intimate.

"I reserved their best table," Jack boasted to Mr. and Mrs. Truman. "That one over there in the corner is the very nicest."

Rebecca frowned. "It looks a little cramped, and it's a *booth*," she said in disgust. "Booths are for people who eat in diners, or for small children. Henry? I would prefer a *real* table."

Henry nodded. He beckoned over Angela, Roberto's oldest daughter. Angela was the manager of the restaurant, and with her waist-length black hair and sparkling dark eyes, she was arguably the most beautiful woman in Sandy Bay.

"Ciao, Bella," Henry said to Angela with a wink. "Tell me, are there any tables left besides that little cramped booth? My gorgeous wife and I would prefer something a bit more...elegant."

Angela smiled graciously. "Si, sir," she breathed, her heavy accent clearly charming Henry. "Let me show you to our private dining space. I believe that will best accommodate you."

When Angela ensured the group was settled in a quiet private dining room, Henry smirked at Jack. "I thought you said that *booth* was the best table in the house," he announced. "Seems like a private dining room is a little more refined, Johnny."

"It's Jack," Jack muttered under his breath as Meghan squeezed his knee beneath the table.

"Now, I wonder what this place has to offer. I hope they have that dish you love Henry. Remember when we had it on our vacation last summer? We stayed in the most beautiful little villa in the Italian countryside, Meghan."

Meghan's smile was strained, but she nodded politely. "That sounds nice, Mama."

Angela returned to the table with four menus, as well as a glass pitcher filled with ice water. "Let me tell you about our special tonight," Angela said. "The lamb is divine; the red sauce atop the platter was made by my father this morning, and I have never tasted anything finer. The fettuccine is the perfect choice for our pasta-enthusiasts, and of course, we have a safer dish for the less adventurous. Our chicken dish is delicious, of course, but for those looking for an experience, I would recommend the lamb or the pasta."

Meghan grinned. "I would love the lamb," she told Angela.

"Excellent. And for your lovely parents?"

Henry handed the menu back to Angela. "We'll take the pasta dish and the lamb; we are going to split both."

Angela beamed. "Fantastico," she said, and then, turning to Jack, "and for you?"

Jack awkwardly gave his menu to Angela. "I'll take the chicken," he murmured as Rebecca's blue eyes grew wide.

"The chicken?" Henry questioned. "We're at a nice place, Johnny. Why don't you try something a little less...bland?"

Jack's cheeks turned red, and Meghan took his hand, bringing it atop the table for all to see. She squeezed it lovingly, but Jack's eyes remained distraught. "He wants chicken, Daddy. It isn't a big deal."

Angela retreated from the dining room, and Rebecca addressed Jack, "I've just never heard of someone ordering *chicken* at a fine dining establishment."

Jack shrugged. "It's my favorite," he muttered.

Rebecca pursed her lips. "Interesting," she offered.

Meghan quickly changed the subject. "Mama, I have some exciting news."

Rebecca's eyes shined. "You've finally joined weight watchers?"

Meghan's face darkened. "No," she whispered.

Henry put his hands up. "Rebecca, you stop that. Our Meghan is perfect. She is the spitting image of my mother, and my mother was a beautiful woman, inside and out."

Rebecca rolled her eyes. "I know you think your mother was perfect," she sighed to her husband. "Meghan? What was your news?"

Meghan sat tall in her seat. "I am going to expand the bakery next year; Truly Sweet has been a massive success, and after some careful thinking, I have decided to add three light lunch options to our menu."

Rebecca clapped her hands in excitement. "That's delightful, dear," she said. "Just make sure you don't indulge too much; I know it can be easy for you to snack when food is around."

Jack put his arm around Meghan. "I'm proud of Meghan for going after her dreams," he declared to the table.

"Jack, just relax," Meghan said to Jack under her breath.

"As are we," Henry countered, placing his arm around his own wife's shoulder. "As Meghan's parents, we only want the *best* for our daughter."

Meghan watched as her father stared into Jack's blue eyes. "I feel like I have the best of everything in my life right now," she assured her parents. "The best boyfriend, the best job, the best friends, and of course, the best family."

Rebecca smiled. "Family truly is the most important thing this time of year. I love spending time with family, and listening to Christmas carols. It's all so magical."

Henry's ears perked up. "Rebecca, do you hear the song playing? It sounds like Bing Crosby's 'White Christmas. Your favorite!"

Rebecca beamed. "Wonderful food, wonderful company, and my favorite carol? This is a truly sweet holiday trip."

An hour and a half later, after Jack and Henry awkwardly fought for the check, the group was escorted out of the restaurant by Roberto Luciano. "Thank you all so much," Roberto gushed as he smiled at Henry, who had left Angela a two-hundred dollar tip. "Your kindness is so appreciated this holiday season."

"The food was just superb," Rebecca declared. "It was to die for. Your restaurant is one of the best I have had the pleasure of visiting."

"It was my idea to come here," Jack chirped as Meghan shot him a dirty look.

"Jack, enough," Meghan whispered. "Just act natural."

"Natural?" Jack asked. "How can I do that when your parents hate me?"

Roberto opened the front door for the Trumans.

"Thank you again. Oh, no. The homeless people."

Meghan saw the group of homeless people sitting on the curb outside of the restaurant. "We can just walk around them," she told Roberto. "It's no big deal."

Roberto shook his head. "I have worked so hard to build the restaurant, and I cannot have these people milling about when I have fine customers dining. You! You there! Shoo."

The man with the Santa beard and headphones lumbered over to Roberto. "Shoo? We ain't dogs, man."

Roberto frowned. "You are worse. Dogs can be taken away and disposed of, but you people never leave."

The homeless man's jaw dropped. "Man, that was uncalled for," he said to Roberto. "We ain't hurting anyone. We're just minding our business."

Roberto clenched his fists. "Mind your business elsewhere!"

The homeless man hung his head. "Man, you ain't got a clue about the reason for this holiday season, do you? Being good to others is what Christmas is about. Would it *kill* you to let us hang here? No. It wouldn't."

Roberto furrowed his brow. "It will *kill* my business. Now, go on. Get. Get out of here before you *kill* my business. Go on! Get out of here, all of you!"

4

"AND JUST SPRINKLE THE SUGAR ON TOP.
Perfect, Meghan. You are such a fast learner."

The morning after having dinner at Luciano's,
Rebecca had appeared at Meghan's front door with a
sack of groceries. "We need to have some mother-
daughter time," she announced to Meghan as she
bustled through the door. "I brought some things
over, and I am going to teach you how to make your
grandmother's famous ginger snap recipe."

"How wonderful," Meghan agreed as she fastened her
favorite monogrammed apron around her neckline.
"Trudy and Pamela are both off today, so we will
have the place all to ourselves."

The two women got to work, with Rebecca mixing
the ingredients together, and Meghan preparing the
utensils. "So, now that it's just us girls, let's have a
little chat," Rebecca suggested as Meghan smiled.

"What do you want to chat about, Mama?" she asked,
tying her long, wavy dark hair into a braid.

Rebecca looked slyly at Meghan. "Jacob Brilander

has become a successful businessman."

Meghan gasped. "Mama, Jacob and I broke up ten years ago. Why are you bringing him up?"

Rebecca's eyes twinkled. "I always loved Jacob," she said wistfully. "He was a nice boy from a good family--an old money family. I just spoke with his mother last week, and she mentioned that he is planning to go into politics! Isn't that exciting?"

Meghan gritted her teeth as she thought of her high school boyfriend. Jacob had been right for her at the time, but when she left Texas for college, they had gone their separate ways. "Mama, I heard Jacob was engaged to a girl he met at school. Morgan something?"

"Didn't last," Rebecca informed her daughter. "That Morgan was too dull, I heard, and Jacob and she broke up before they even walked down the aisle."

Meghan shuddered. "Mama, this is none of my business. I haven't thought of him in years. Why are you telling me this?"

Rebecca gently put the ingredients to the side and looked Meghan in the eyes. "Meghan, you aren't getting any younger," she began. "And this John fellow doesn't seem to be serious about you."

Meghan's dark eyes filled with tears at her mother's nagging. "It's Jack, Mama," she said. "Jack. And he is serious about me. He loves me."

Rebecca shrugged. "I don't see a ring on your finger…."

Meghan placed her hands on her hips. "We've only been boyfriend and girlfriend for *months*, Mama!"

Rebecca shook her head. "Your Daddy and I only dated for two months before we were engaged, Meghan. When you know, you *know*, and I just don't see the sparks between the two of you."

Meghan felt the heat rising to her face, but she did not want to argue with her mother. She quietly wiped her hands on her apron and returned to work on the ginger snaps.

"Meghan?"

Meghan felt her mother's hand on her shoulder. "Meghan, when are you coming home to Texas? You've been away too long. You told me that you would move home if things in Hollywood didn't work out, and yet, here you are, frittering away in a bakery."

Meghan's stomach sank. "Mama," she quietly protested. "I work hard here. I am the *owner*. Sure, it isn't glitzy or glamorous, but I'm happy in Sandy Bay. I'm happy with Jack."

Rebecca closed her eyes and leaned against the wall, dramatically fanning her face. "I just don't understand," she told her daughter. "You were a debutante, Meghan. You are from a good family, you have an education, and you could easily come home with Daddy and me to Texas. Your brothers and sisters would love to see you, and I could arrange tea with Jacob and his mother…"

Meghan threw the wooden spoon she had been using on the floor. She was shocked at her own outburst; Meghan was usually a gentle, sweet woman, but now, with her own mother dismissing her successes, she felt a flutter of anger move from her belly to her head.

"What has gotten into you?" Rebecca asked her daughter as she stared at the spoon in horror. "Meghan that is not how you behave."

Meghan clenched her jaw. "Mama, I like my life here. I love my boyfriend. I am *not* going back to Texas. You have to let me live my life, Mama. You have to let me make my own choices and chase my own dreams."

Rebecca removed the apron from her neck and folded it, placing it neatly on the counter. She walked to Meghan and planted a long, motherly kiss on her forehead. "I'll just let you work," she murmured as she collected her purse and moved to the door. "You seem….tired. I think it's best if you collected yourself, and then we can spend time together later."

Meghan said nothing as Rebecca turned to blow her a kiss. "Just think about it, Sugar," she insisted as she waved goodbye. "Just think about coming home."

Later that evening, Meghan and Jack were relaxing at Eight Ball, the pool bar frequented by the local police officers. Meghan was fantastic at pool, and she and

Jack had made plans earlier in the week to play a few games.

"I'm so glad we get to hang out tonight," she told Jack as she reared back her arm and then shot the ball forward. "Eight Ball is such a fun place to relax, and it doesn't hurt that I've been schooling you in pool!"

Jack did not laugh, and Meghan nervously bit her bottom lip. "Are you having fun?" she asked him as she shot another ball. "Your friends are over there. Should we go say hi?"

Jack shook his head. "Honestly, Meghan, I'm not in the mood to stay here anymore. What you said when we walked in really bugged me, and I think we should call it a night."

Meghan wracked her brain, frantically trying to think of what she and Jack had spoken about when they first arrived at the bar. "Are you talking about the conversation I had with my mother today?" she asked him worriedly. "I thought it was kind of annoying, but kind of funny. I just wanted to fill you in."

Jack looked down at his pool stick.

"Jack?" she asked. "What's wrong?"

Jack grimaced. "It really irks me that your Mom brought up your ex," he admitted to her.

"Jack, I dated Jacob in high school," she protested, placing a hand on Jack's heart. "I love *you*."

He softly pushed her hand away. "It just doesn't feel great that despite my efforts, your parents want you to leave me, and to leave Sandy Bay."

Meghan pursed her lips, unsure of how to respond to her beloved boyfriend. He was *right*; he had tried his best to win over the Trumans, but Meghan's parents were hardly giving Jack the time of day. Meghan did not know what to do; she wanted her family to adore her loyal, loving, boyfriend as much as she did, but with their eyes on Jacob Brilander, the Trumans would never see Jack for the amazing man he was.

"Look, they just need time to warm up to you," she pleaded. "I'm sorry I mentioned the conversation with my Mom to you. I didn't mean to upset you, Jack. I would never want to upset you."

Jack placed the pool stick beneath the table. "I think we should just go, Meghan. I don't feel like hanging out any more."

Meghan followed Jack's lead, placing her pool stick in a rack beneath the table. She walked behind him as he left the bar, and they walked toward the bakery in silence. When they reached the front door, Jack leaned in and kissed Meghan on her cheek.

"Not a real kiss?" Meghan asked as she stared up at her boyfriend.

Jack hesitated. "I just don't feel great," he told her. "I think we should just say goodnight. I'll call you tomorrow."

Meghan stared as Jack turned around and began walking away from her. "Jack? Please? Come back."

Jack did not turn around, and as he trudged through the snow that covered the sidewalk, Meghan felt as though her heart had turned to ice.

5

THE NEXT MORNING, Meghan's spirits were lifted when Karen Denton, her dear friend, walked into the bakery. Karen had been Meghan's neighbor when they both lived in Los Angeles, and Karen had been the one to convince Meghan to move to Sandy Bay. Despite being in her early seventies, Karen was the most adventurous, active person Meghan knew, and she always managed to put a smile on Meghan's face.

"How fabulous to see you," Karen greeted her. "I just left my spin class, and I wanted to stop by and see if your folks were around. It's not everyday that your dear friend's family is in town."

Meghan smiled and said, "They are upstairs in my apartment visiting with the dogs. I'll go get them."

She returned with her parents in tow, each holding one of Meghan's dogs. "Karen, these are my parents," she announced as Rebecca and Henry smiled at Karen.

"Oh, it is a pleasure to meet you at last," Karen shouted joyfully as she gathered Rebecca into her arms. "Meghan is a doll, and I try to look after her here. She is such a good girl; she really has a good head on her shoulders! But you both know that, of course."

Rebecca gently pulled away from Karen and smiled. "The pleasure is ours. Meghan says you watch out for her here in town. Thank you for being somewhat of a surrogate mother to our girl."

Karen turned to Henry. "And you! Meghan's father? What a thrill."

Henry grinned. "We are pleased to meet you, Karen. It's been so nice meeting Meghan's friends in Sandy Bay."

Karen turned to Meghan and winked. "And what did your folks think of sweet Jack? What a catch he is."

Henry and Rebecca raised their eyebrows, and Karen caught the looks on their faces. "You two have met Jack?"

Rebecca nodded. "We have," she confirmed. "He's...nice."

Karen placed her hands on her hips. "He is more than nice," she countered. "Jack Irvin is one of the most darling boys in this town. He was just promoted to detective, which is a huge deal. He also volunteers with the youth club in town, and he once saved the Minister's dog that was caught on the railway tracks!"

Henry looked at Meghan, his own dark eyes wide. "We've probably been giving him too hard of a time," he muttered as Meghan nodded emphatically. "Rebecca and I just want the best for our little girl."

"Jack is the best," Karen explained to Meghan's parents. "If I had a daughter living in Sandy Bay, I would give my right arm to have her dating such a good boy."

Rebecca frowned. "Maybe we've been too hard on him," she told her husband. "Karen here says that he is wonderful, and if Meghan really likes him…."

Henry nodded vigorously. "We'll make things right with him. Meghan, I'm sorry; I've been missing my dogs at home, and that's put me in a foul mood. I'll make things right with your man, and I'll get back to being myself."

Meghan beamed. "Thanks, Daddy. I didn't realize you were missing your dogs so much. Why don't we go take my dogs out for a walk together? Fiesta and Siesta would love a little walk with their Grandpa."

Henry smiled. "That sounds perfect, Sugar."

Meghan strapped the dogs into their harnesses. She gave one leash to her father, and as they walked out the front door, she asked her mother, "Are you and Karen okay to visit with each other for a bit?"

Rebecca's eyes twinkled. "Karen and I are getting on quite well," she informed her daughter. "We will be chatting away. You two have fun."

Meghan and Henry stepped outside into the cold

winter air. Fiesta and Siesta shivered; their hair was short, and Meghan wished that they had coats as warm as hers for the chilly Pacific Northwest winter.

"This is just like when we took walks together when you were a little girl," Henry shared as he and Meghan walked the dogs along the snowy sidewalk. "Of course, we didn't have snow in Texas, but you and I would always go for long walks together with the dogs. Do you remember the dogs we had when you were little? You just loved Dave, the Great Dane we had. He used to sleep with you every night! Your brothers and sisters were always so jealous that he loved you best."

Meghan smiled. "I remember Dave," she told her father as they turned a corner, a flurry of snowflakes came sprinkling down. "I loved our walks together, Daddy. With such a big family, it was special to have alone time with you and Mama."

Henry's eyes filled with tears. "You are just growing up so fast, Meghan," he lamented to his daughter. "I can't believe my little girl is old enough to live so far from home, or own her own business, or even have a boyfriend."

"Hey!"

Meghan and Henry turned to see Jack walking toward them, in his arms, a bouquet of red roses.

"Speak of the devil," Henry muttered as Jack approached them.

"Meghan," Jack began as he stared into Meghan's dark eyes. "I'm sorry I was upset. I'm sorry, and I was coming over to apologize and to bring you these flowers."

Before Meghan could speak, she heard her father clear his throat. Henry looked into Jack's eyes and reached out for his hand. "Jack," he began. "I want to apologize for not being the kindest while my wife and I have been here. Meghan is our little girl, and we want only the best for her. It's clear that you make her happy, and that you've helped her settle here in Sandy Bay. That said, I want to thank you for taking care of my girl."

Jack's eyes widened. "Thank you, sir," he said to Henry. "That means a lot to me."

Henry shook Jack's hand. "Let me make it all up to you. I want to take you two to dinner tonight at Luciano's; their food was just incredible, and I want to start fresh. Can we do that?"

Jack grinned. "Of course," he told Henry. "Well, only if Meghan is up for it. Meghan? Can you forgive me? Can we all start fresh?"

Meghan blushed, aware that her father was watching. "Yes," she whispered to Jack as she leaned up on her tiptoes to kiss him gently on the lips. "Let's start fresh."

That evening, as Henry, Rebecca, Jack, and Meghan stepped out of Henry's rental car and onto the snowy streets, Meghan gasped as she caught sight of a commotion outside of the restaurant.

"What is going on?"

Jack gently tucked Meghan behind him and turned to Henry. "Mr. Truman, I am going to see what's going on," he said as he surveyed the scene. "It looks like a crowd of homeless folks is rioting. Meghan, stay with your father. I will be right back."

Jack returned moments later with a weary look in his blue eyes. "What happened?" Meghan asked her boyfriend as he shook his head. "Jack?"

Jack sighed. "One of the homeless fellows is dead. That guy we saw last time with the Santa beard? I just cleared the area, and he was lying on the ground. I took his pulse, but he's gone. I called for backup and an ambulance, so it's about to get pretty busy here. I have to stay on the scene, for a few minutes, but then I can drive you all back. Henry? Will you please keep an eye on Meghan? I don't want anything to happen to her."

Henry nodded. "Of course I will keep my baby girl safe," he declared. "Come on, Meghan. Stay close to me. This place is brimming with trouble."

6

"I'M SO UPSET, I can hardly think straight," Rebecca lamented as Jack silently wound through the snowy streets to take the Trumans back to their hotel. "First a riot, and now, a man is dead? Meghan, what kind of town is this?"

Meghan said nothing. She stared at the window, and shivered as she saw two homeless men outside of Spark. She wondered how they were staying warm in the frigid evening, and she pulled her coat tightly around her.

"Well, here we are," Jack announced as he turned onto the circular driveway outside of the hotel. "I'll walk you in."

"I'll wait in the car," Meghan told her parents as they unbuckled their seatbelts.

"Not a chance," Henry said. "There was a riot and a death tonight....you are coming inside with us."

Meghan frowned, but obeyed her father. She stepped out of the car and sidled up to Jack, looping her elbow through his.

"I am just flabbergasted," Rebecca complained as they entered the luxurious hotel lobby. "Meghan, I do not feel comfortable with you living in such a place."

"Let's discuss this later, Mama," Meghan grumbled as Lewis Templeton, the hotel manager, hurried over to the Trumans. In his fitted white suit and pointed leather shoes, Lewis was the epitome of elegance; he was known in town for having fine taste, and while Meghan didn't know him well, she sensed there was more to him than met the eye.

"Good evening," Lewis cooed. "You must be the Trumans, my newest guests? It is a pleasure to serve you at our finest establishment. I'm Lewis Templeton, the manager of this hotel."

Henry nodded brusquely. "Thanks," he told Lewis.

Lewis leaned in and took Rebecca's hands. "Mrs. Truman? You look upset, and we never want our dear guests to feel upset in our hotel. Is there something I can bring for you? A coffee? A vitamin water? A scone?"

Rebecca shook her head. "Forgive me," she said to Lewis. "I've had the most upsetting evening."

Lewis wrinkled his forehead. "Oh? May I ask why?"

Rebecca scowled. "Those homeless men….they were camped outside of Luciano's, and..."

Lewis' face darkened. "Were they causing trouble again? I had a group of them with the nerve to stay outside of this hotel. You can bet your bottom dollar I had them sent away. I am so sorry you were disturbed, Mrs. Truman. I've told the mayor a million times that we must take care of our homeless problem in Sandy Bay!"

Rebecca smiled weakly. "I appreciate your concern," she breathed. "Mr. Templeton, it was a pleasure to meet you. Henry, take me upstairs. I need a stiff drink, and I need it now."

The next day, Meghan met her mother at Crumpet, a tea shop on the west side of town.

"I just think you should consider your safety, Meghan," Rebecca lectured as the mother and daughter sipped tea together. "You are a young woman living on your own in a town filled with trouble."

Meghan disagreed. "Sandy Bay isn't filled with trouble," she told her mother. "It's filled with kind, caring people who are passionate about making our little town the best it can be. Look! Over there. It's Kirsty Fisher. She is one of Sandy Bay's biggest philanthropists and organizers. You should meet her,

Mama. Kirsty!"

Kirsty smiled her perfectly white teeth at Rebecca and Meghan and flitted over, an organic green tea in her hand. "Meghan, what a pleasure. I was just going over plans for that poor homeless man's funeral with the junior leader of the City Committee. There's no one else to plan it, and we feel everyone in Sandy Bay deserves to be honored when they pass."

Meghan gritted her teeth. She did not want to discuss the death with Kirsty and her mother; she had hoped Kirsty's enthusiasm for Sandy Bay could sway her mother, and she tried to change the subject.

"That's nice, Kirsty, but tell me, what *other* projects are you working on for the city these days?"

Kirsty bit her lip. "Well, my charity is partnering with the local department store," she told Meghan and Rebecca. "We scout out people to play Santa during the holiday season."

"How lovely," Rebecca cooed. "That sounds like great fun."

"It is," Kirsty agreed. "But it's a bit sad this year; we work with the homeless population to find the perfect Santa; the department store offers one lucky person employment as Santa for the season, and then they receive a twenty-five thousand dollar prize to help them get back on their feet after the holidays are over."

"Twenty-five thousand dollars?" Meghan exclaimed.

Kirsty nodded. "It's such a sweet opportunity for someone to turn their life around. It's just tinged with sadness this year; that man who was killed? He was one of our finalists this year. He came to the audition with a Santa beard and such a wonderful spirit. He received a standing ovation, and he was down to the top three in the competition. The selection committee was very pleased with him, and rumor was that they were going to announce his selection this week. Now, we'll never see him rise up; I'm planning his funeral instead of his congratulatory tea."

Rebecca cocked her head to the side. "I don't believe we've met," she informed Kirsty. "I'm Meghan's mother. And, you are?"

Kirsty flashed her perfect smile at Rebecca and tossed her blonde hair. "I'm Kirsty Fisher," she said to Rebecca. "I live for Sandy Bay events; I adore this town with all of my heart, and Meghan has been such a doll in helping with several of my affairs."

Rebecca studied Kirsty, and then, she smiled at her. "I enjoy your passion," she told Kirsty. "Now, sit down. Let's chat. Tell me more about the man who died?"

Meghan cringed. She knew her mother was prying in order to persuade Meghan to leave Sandy Bay, and she wished Kirsty would stop discussing the deceased homeless man.

"It's terribly sad," Kirsty lamented as Rebecca listened with raised eyebrows. "His name was Roger

Williams, and he used to be quite the successful Sandy Bay resident. He was a business owner, and from what I hear, an avid volunteer in the community."

Rebecca ran a hand through her blonde hair. "How did his life spiral out of control?"
Meghan gasped. "Mother! That's so rude."

"What?" Rebecca asked. "I'm just asking. Obviously something had to have gone wrong to have a successful businessman lose everything and end up on the streets."

Kirsty bobbed her head up and down. "From what I've been told, Roger's life took a tumble; he went through a nasty divorce, and that just sent him barreling downhill. Roger became paranoid and crazy, and he went in and out of mental hospitals for years. His poor ex-wife finally took his children and left town. Roger then ran out of money, and a few years ago, he was in jail for robbing a grocery store. The authorities determined he was only stealing food and they let him out after a few nights. From what I've been told, he went back to the mental hospital, was given the proper medication, and then, he had a good few years."

"Then what happened?" Meghan asked, caught up in the story.

"He was given a free apartment to live in, as well as a part-time job," Kirsty explained. "But then, it all went downhill again, and he spiraled out of control. Word on the street is that he finally got help a few months ago, which is the only reason why we could have considered him for the part of Santa. He had a social worker, a therapist, and a case manager, and he was finally doing well."

"And now, he's dead," Meghan whispered sadly.

"He's gone, and we'll have to use our second-choice Santa," Kirsty said in disgust. "Oh, I didn't mean it like that," she said, seeing Meghan's look of horror. "It's just that Roger was so wonderful, and I thought he would do a great job."

"I've been auditioning for forty-seven years, and I've never been selected."

The three women turned to see Mrs. Sally Sheridan hobbling toward them on her cane. Mrs. Sheridan was an elderly woman who had previously loathed Meghan, but after she had come to Mrs. Sheridan's side during a town protest, the pair had become friendly. Mrs. Sheridan was still known for being fussy and hard to please, but Meghan's heart was softening toward the old woman.

"Mrs. Sheridan," Kirsty greeted her as she maneuvered her way to the table. "It's lovely to see you."

"Yeah, yeah," she grumbled. "I heard you three talking about the Santa auditions. I've been auditioning for years, and I feel like I've never been given a fair shot."

Kirsty pursed her lips. "The role is for Santa Clause,"

she explained patiently to Mrs. Sheridan. "Santa Clause is a man, Mrs. Sheridan, and you are not a man."

Mrs. Sheridan glared at Kirsty. "That just doesn't seem very progressive of you," she argued. "I'm sure my Santa voice is better than any man's, and I sure have a big belly for the kids to sit on. Just look at it."

Rebecca gasped as Mrs. Sheridan stroked her large, overweight belly. Meghan and Kirsty were used to Mrs. Sheridan's occasional crass remarks, but prim, proper Rebecca Truman did not know how to handle Sally Sheridan.

"Look," Kirsty said to Mrs. Sheridan. "I'm sorry you haven't been selected. I truly appreciate your eagerness to participate and make the children happy as Santa."

Mrs. Sheridan rolled her eyes. "I don't care about the children," she explained to Kirsty. "I care about the money, as well as gaining exposure as an actress. I was born for the stage, Kirsty."

Kirsty sighed. "You are the most dramatic woman in town," she muttered.

"What?" Mrs. Sheridan roared. "Do I need to turn up my hearing aid?"

Kirsty slapped a smile back on her face. "No," she said gently. "Just keep trying out each year, Mrs. Sheridan! You never know what can happen."

Mrs. Sheridan grumbled as she hobbled out of the tea shop. Kirsty looked to Rebecca. "She is an odd duck," Kirsty said apologetically to Rebecca. "But it isn't just her; others have gotten bent out of shape because of the silly Santa competition."

Meghan raised an eyebrow. "What do you mean?"

Kirsty shook her head. "We get so many complaints during the round where we make cuts," she explained to Meghan and Rebecca. "When we send out the notices to tell people that they didn't make it to the next round, they get so angry. We've gotten threats before! It's wild. People would *kill* for the role of Santa."

Meghan bit her bottom lip. "*Kill* for the *role* of Santa, huh? I'm sure it's fun to play Santa, but I'm sure that twenty-five thousand dollar prize attached is something people would be a little more inclined to kill for. I wonder if that had anything to do with Roger's death. You said that he was known to be a top finalist?"

Kirsty nodded. "I hadn't even thought that the contest could be connected to his death," she said to Meghan. "Oh my. How terrible to think of."

Rebecca narrowed her eyes at her daughter. "This charming little town seems a little darker after hearing this, Meghan. I'm just not quite sure how I feel about you staying in Sandy Bay, especially after this information. I think it's time you come home to Texas, and I don't want to hear another peep of an argument about it!"

7

THE NEXT MORNING, Meghan was pleasantly surprised to find Jack at her doorstep before the bakery opened. She wasn't expecting him, and as she peered out the window to see him smiling back at her, she hoped that her messy hair and sleepy eyes wouldn't dissuade him from giving her a good morning kiss.

"Hey there, handsome," she cheerfully greeted her boyfriend as she unlocked the doors. "This is a surprise."

Jack leaned down to kiss Meghan softly on the lips. Meghan felt a shiver run up her spine; she and Jack had been dating for several months now, but it still felt magical when he kissed her.

"To what do I owe this pleasure?" she playfully asked as Jack pulled away. "Would you like some breakfast? It's well before our opening time, but you know I would happily whip something up for you."

Jack shook his head. "I just got off my night shift," he told Meghan as she noticed the dark bags under his eyes. "There's been a break in the case; we have a few suspects, but a new addition to the suspect list has me shaken."

Meghan's dark eyes widened. "Who is it?"

Jack sighed. "Mr. Luciano is on the list," he informed her. "The police think that maybe he was just tired of all of the homeless folks outside of the restaurant. You heard how upset he was that day we had dinner with your folks."

Meghan gasped. Mr. Luciano had always been kind to her, and she could hardly believe that he was an official suspect. "Are you sure? Do they know how Roger died, yet?"

Jack frowned. "That was the other disturbing news of my night shift," he muttered. "Roger died from something he ate; how easy it would have been for Roberto to throw out some food for those people to gobble up, and now...someone is dead."

Meghan bit her lip. She recalled the conversation she and her mother had had with Kirsty the day before, and she wagged her finger in protest. "I don't know, Jack," Meghan said. "It just seems too crazy. Mr. Luciano didn't want his restaurant to be plagued with crowds of homeless people out front, but I don't see him killing someone. What about one of Roger's friends? The group of people there looked pretty rough; what if another homeless person killed him?"

Jack shrugged. "I brought that up to Chief Nunan," he murmured. "You said yourself when we spoke last night on the phone that Roger was set to win that department store gig; perhaps someone was angry about it and killed him."

Meghan nodded. "That's what I think. I think rumor was that Roger was going to win the role as Santa, as well as the money, and some sore loser decided to take away the opportunity permanently."

"I floated that idea to the Chief," Jack breathed. "But she wouldn't hear it; she is fixated on Roberto right now. Anyway, I wanted to let you know the news. I need to head home and get some sleep."

Meghan turned on her heel and dashed to the kitchen, returning with a large disposable cup filled with steaming coffee. "For you," she announced as she presented the coffee to Jack. "A large caramel macchiato made with my special homemade whipped cream."

Jack accepted the cup and bent down to kiss Meghan on the forehead. "You are an angel," he told his girlfriend. "Thank you for taking such good care of me."

Meghan reached out to give Jack a playful swat on the bottom. "Now get out of here," she ordered him with a smile on her face. "You need some sleep, Mister!"

****

"That isn't your color, Meghan. Didn't you listen earlier when I told you that?" Rebecca chided as Meghan stepped out of the dressing room at Spark.

Jackie nodded in agreement. "I think she's right," she told Meghan. "That bright orange just doesn't work with your hair."

Meghan politely smiled at her mother and friend, but as she retreated to the dressing room, she scowled. She had been convinced by her mother to go shopping for the afternoon, and while she had at first thought that bringing Jackie along would soften her mother's harsh comments, she was incorrect; Rebecca and Jackie had bonded instantly, and they were constantly teaming up against Meghan.

"I can't believe she chose that sweater," Meghan heard her mother murmur to Jackie. "She and I are just built so differently, and she doesn't seem to understand that with those...womanly looks, she needs to gravitate toward the neutrals."

"I agree," Jackie told Rebecca and Meghan's stomach churned. "Meghan has such a pretty face, but you cannot wear orange with those curves. I wish she would hit the gym with me every once in awhile. I ask her, Rebecca, but she usually turns me down."

Meghan marched out of the dressing room in her

black camisole, her arms crossed across her chest. "I can hear every word you two are saying," she told her mother and Jackie as she shivered, the hair on her arms sticking straight up. "Mama, I wish I were itty bitty like you, but I am not. I know I'm not the most stylish, but I try."

Rebecca rolled her eyes. "Don't do a pity party," she said dismissively to Meghan. "Why don't you just pack up your things and move home to Texas? I can help you open a bakery there, and I can hire a stylist for you. You'll be the talk of the town, Meghan! You could blow every little cafe and bakery out of the water. Your father and I could help you turn Truly Sweet into a franchise!"

Meghan balled her hands into fists. "I don't want to go home to Texas," she declared as Jackie walked away to browse a rack of sweaters on the other side of the store. "Mama, I've told you repeatedly that I am happy here. Why isn't that enough for you?"

Rebecca sighed. "Someday you will understand," she said as Meghan stared at her. "When you have a daughter, you will only want the best for her."

"The best for her is Sandy Bay, you silly goose."

Meghan and Rebecca turned to find Sally Sheridan hobbling toward them, her cane scraping the trendy chestnut-colored wooden floor of the boutique as she wandered closer. "Meghan belongs in Sandy Bay. She lives here. She loves it here. *We* love her here. She turned that bakery of hers into a success, she's dating the best boy in town, and she makes everyone here happy with her big smile and good spirits."

Tears welled in Meghan's eyes. She and Mrs. Sheridan had grown closer over the last few months, but she never dreamed that Mrs. Sheridan would have such lovely things to say about her. She wiped a tear from her cheeks and walked to Mrs. Sheridan with outstretched arms, eager to embrace the old woman.

"What are you doing?" Mrs. Sheridan asked in alarm as Meghan drew closer. She waved her cane at Meghan's head. "Back up, missy."

"I just want to give you a little hug," she laughed as Mrs. Sheridan stared at her. "Your words touched my heart, and I wanted to give you a squeeze to thank you."

Mrs. Sheridan shook her head. "No, no, no," she said, firmly planting her cane in front of her. "I'm not in a sappy mood today. I'm just telling the truth. The truth is that you belong here, and your mother needs to get off of her high horse and let you be about it. You hear me?"

Rebecca looked startled to be addressed in such a brusque manner, but before she could respond, Mrs. Sheridan began to hobble away. Before she walked outside, she turned back around to shout, "even though Meghan's treats gave me diarrhea once, they are still the best in the Pacific Northwest."

Meghan's face burned with shame; she knew that her treats had never made anyone sick, and she was embarrassed that Mrs. Sheridan had shouted that across the fashionable boutique. Meghan watched as Mrs. Sheridan exited the store, and then leaned down to settle into an overstuffed purple armchair. "That was a lot," she sighed to her mother. "I'm sorry she was a bit rude."

Rebecca looked down at her high heels and then looked back at Meghan, a look of shame on her face. "I'm sorry," she whispered to Meghan. "You and I have always been so different, and I have always pushed you too hard. I'm sorry I've been pushing for you to come home. To be honest, Meghan, your Daddy and I miss you. We would like you to be nearby. You're missing so much, Meghan; your brothers and sisters are getting older, and we just want you to be a bigger part of our lives."

Meghan pursed her lips. "I have to live my own life, Mama," she said softly as a black tear of mascara raced down Rebecca's cheek.

"I know," Rebecca replied. "And it seems like you live a good life here. Everyone has such lovely things to say about you. You've really made an impression here."

Meghan smiled. "I love it here."

"I can see why," she said. "The people are kind, the shops and restaurants are adorable, and the sight of the ocean nearby is just good for the soul."

Meghan sighed. "I wish you and Daddy could just live here part of the time," she lamented.

Rebecca stared into her eyes. "What if we could?"

Meghan raised an eyebrow. "What do you mean? Texas is so far away."

Rebecca laughed. "In this age, nothing is far away; we have endless airline miles from Daddy's business, and we have been thinking about investing in some property. What if we added a place in Sandy Bay to our list?"

Meghan jumped up and down in excitement. "Really? That would be wonderful. I love you two so much and would love to see more of you. I know just the person who could help you out! My friend, Kayley, is the best real estate agent around. If you are serious about a place here, she will go all out to help."

Rebecca leaned forward and kissed her daughter on the forehead, leaving a smudge of pale pink lipstick on Meghan's skin. "I am serious," she whispered as she hugged her daughter. "I am serious about moving to Sandy Bay."

8

"THIS IS A CUTE OFFICE," Rebecca gushed as Meghan led her inside of the local real estate company. "I just love that waterfall in the corner; the aesthetics here are fantastic."

"Thank you, I designed the place myself," said Kayley Kane, one of Sandy Bay's best agents.

She effortlessly strutted across the room, her tall high heels making her legs look like skyscrapers. Kayley and Meghan were friendly; they had been thrown together for various events in town, and today, as Meghan imagined her mother and father buying a second house in Sandy Bay, Meghan was elated to see her real estate agent friend.

"Kayley, good to see you," Meghan said as she gestured her mother to sit beside her in the expensive chairs facing Kayley's desk. "This is my mother, Rebecca Truman. Mama and my Daddy are looking to maybe find a second home in Sandy Bay."

Meghan watched as Kayley's eyes scanned Rebecca's outfit and purse; Kayley was known for having expensive taste, and Meghan was sure she would recognize Rebecca's designer sweater and matching handbag. Kayley leaned forward in her chair and clasped her red-finger nailed hands in front of her nose. "I would be honored to help Mr. and Mrs. Truman in their search. Mrs. Truman, what exactly is your budget for a second home in Sandy Bay?"

Rebecca laughed. "Surely it isn't proper to first discuss finances," she lightheartedly chastised Kayley. "Let's just say Meghan's Daddy and I have enough to be comfortable here."

Kayley's eyes widened. "Of course," she said, twirling a strand of freshly-dyed auburn hair around her finger. "Forgive me. Let's talk about your lifestyle. How will you and your family be using a new property?"

Rebecca pursed her lips. "Well, Meghan's Daddy won't be around often; his work keeps him very busy. It would mostly be me here. I would like to have things to do while I am in town; I love throwing charity events and parties, but I wouldn't mind having a shop to duck into, either."

Kayley's eyes sparkled. "We have a lot of properties that offer space for hosting events," she told Rebecca. "And we even have some commercial properties for purchase. You could easily scoop up one of the buildings or lots downtown and run a little shop. What about a flower shop? You could open a flower shop and check in on it while you are here."

Rebecca smiled warmly. "That's a sweet little idea," she said. "I'm not sure how I feel about getting my hands dirty, though. Let's just talk about residential options."

Kayley nodded and rose from her seat behind the desk. "Of course. Excuse me for one moment, and I will go find some pamphlets detailing your options."

As Kayley marched away, Meghan glanced over her shoulder to see a crowd of people sitting angrily in the lobby. "What's going on out there?" Meghan asked as she fidgeted in her seat.

"Ugh, that dead man just ruined so many of our deals," Kayley chirped as she walked back into her office. "I was just about to sell the property next to Luciano's, but because that guy dropped dead there, no one wants it. All of those people out there are trying to cancel deals and property purchases we had signed on. It's madness."

Meghan's eyes widened. "All of those people want to give up on their property deals because that fellow died?"

Kayley rolled her eyes. "I know, it's ridiculous. I'm going to lose out on so much money because of this. I wish that man would have had the courtesy to drop dead elsewhere. My son's tuition bill is coming up soon, and I need the cash to pay for the private school. My ex-husband isn't helping with anything anymore, so this whole debacle makes my life more difficult."

Meghan tried to empathize, but she was disheartened by Kayley's disdain for Roger Williams.

"Kayley," she said softly. "I'm sorry it's stressful, but what about public school? I hear the schools here are great. Couldn't your son go to one of the public schools? You could save so much money."

Kayley narrowed her eyes at Meghan and gestured at a framed photograph of her son. "My little boy deserves the best," she hissed. "Maybe you'll understand when you are a mother someday."

Rebecca uncrossed her legs and picked up her leather handbag. She rose to her feet and beckoned to Meghan to follow suit. "I think it's time we go," she said to Kayley as she tucked her blonde hair behind her ears. "Ms. Kane, we can schedule a showing for next week. It seems best if we get out of your hair; this place looks crowded, and we don't want to take up too much of your time."

Kayley's face was panicked as Rebecca and Meghan walked to the door. "Wait!" she exclaimed. "I apologize for my outburst; I just care deeply about my son, and I don't want to miss an opportunity to help you find your dream home in Sandy Bay, Mrs. Truman."

Rebecca nodded politely. "We'll surely find time to work together later in the week," she told Kayley. "For now, we'll leave you be. Have a nice day, Ms. Kane."

As Meghan and Rebecca left the office, Rebecca sighed. "That woman was impossibly rude," she huffed to Meghan. "Didn't you say you are friendly with her? Really, Meghan, you need to surround yourself with good company if you want to become your best self."

Meghan shrugged. "Kayley and I are friendly, but she isn't my best friend, Mama," she explained. "Besides, she's the best agent in town; she'll do a great job helping you and Daddy find a place. Just give her a chance."

Meghan and Rebecca rounded the corner and found Angela Luciano outside walking a small Italian greyhound. "Angela, so good to see you," Meghan exclaimed. "Is that your dog? He is so cute. We should get together for a doggie playdate sometime."

Angela flashed her bright smile at Meghan and Rebecca before bending down to stroke the mottled gray greyhound behind the ears. "Yes," she breathed in her thick Italian accent. "This is Sarzana. He's my precious bambino. He loves other dogs, and I'm sure he would love your little loves."

Rebecca beamed at Angela. "It's so nice to see you out and about," she gushed as Angela stood beside her dog. "Meghan and I were just out visiting Kayley Kane. I'm looking for a second home here."

"That's wonderful," Angela cooed. "Sandy Bay is a darling town. When my family moved here from Italy when I was a teenager, we were welcomed with open arms. You will make many happy memories in Sandy Bay."

Rebecca tossed her hair behind her shoulder. "I'm just hoping to find the perfect house and the perfect set of activities," she explained to Angela. "It's very important to get connected with the right people and events, and I hope to contribute to Sandy Bay since my daughter loves it so much."

Angela's face brightened. "Are you interested in charities? Our restaurant is connected with many of the local organizations. I could give you some contacts if you are interested."

"I would adore that," Rebecca gushed. "You are just so beautiful and lovely, Angela. Thank you so much."

"Of course," she replied. "In fact, tomorrow, our restaurant is partnering with a charity that gives meals to the homeless. I joke with my father that we give the homeless enough meals, as they dig through our dumpster each night. But all jokes aside, this charity is a good one, and we are pleased to partake. Would you two like to join us tomorrow? Give back this holiday season?"

Meghan shook her head. "Sorry, Angela," she said as Rebecca glared at her. "I have a busy schedule tomorrow, and I put off some of my baking to go out with my mother today. Maybe next time?"

Rebecca gave Meghan a stern look. "That is not in the spirit, Meghan," she whispered to her daughter. "If you want me to be part of this town so badly, then we are going to go volunteer with beautiful Angela. Understood?"

Meghan bit her lip, upset that her mother had spoken to her like a child. "Understood," she muttered as

Rebecca's frown turned into a glamorous smile. "*Understood*, Mama."

9

THAT EVENING, MEGHAN INVITED Pamela and Trudy to the bakery to meet her mother. Concerned by Kayley's rudeness, Rebecca had insisted meeting some of Meghan's other Sandy Bay friends.

"I want to make sure that my daughter is spending time with the right people," she told her daughter as they prepared for the girls' night at Truly Sweet. "This will be fun, Meghan. I'm going to teach you all one of my favorite recipes. They will all love it, and we can spend even more time together."

"That's just what we need," Meghan groaned as Rebecca fastened an apron around her neck to protect her vintage Chanel sweater. "More time together."

Rebecca turned to smile at her daughter. "What did you say?"

Meghan shook her head. "Nothing, Mama. Oh, look. Trudy and Pamela are here."

Rebecca smiled graciously as Meghan's two employees walked into the bakery. "Hello! I am Meghan's mother, Rebecca. It's a pleasure to meet you ladies."

Pamela, Meghan's high school-aged employee, was brimming with excitement. "Nice to meet you. Meghan didn't tell us you were so glamorous!"

Rebecca waved a hand to dismiss Pamela's compliment, but Meghan knew her mother was pleased by the teenager's words. "And Mom, this is Trudy," Meghan said as she introduced her middle-aged employee to her mother. Trudy looked frumpy compared to Rebecca; both women were approximately the same age, but with her lumpy holiday sweater, frizzy hair, and knee-length wool skirt, Trudy looked ages older than the refined Rebecca.

"Let's get started with our baking," Rebecca instructed the group as she gestured to the ingredients and utensils she had laid out. "I've done a little prep, and I'm excited to teach you girls."

"Girls?" Trudy murmured. "I'm fifty-five years old, and I've been in the kitchen before."

"I'm just being silly," Rebecca laughed. "Come on, Trudy, get in the spirit!"

The four women got to work. Meghan turned on a holiday radio station, and the sounds of classical Christmas music filled the room. Everyone was in a pleasant mood, and Trudy lit one of the peppermint candles in the kitchen, giving the space a warm, festive glow and smell.

After nearly two hours of holiday fun, out of nowhere, the atmosphere shifted. "No, no, no!" Rebecca screeched as Pamela twisted a thick piece of yellow dough. "That is not the correct shape."

Meghan's dark eyes widened as she looked at the dough. Pamela had spun the pieces into an intricate braid, and Meghan was impressed with the shape and texture of the dough. "Mama," Meghan protested. "Pamela's braid is so pretty. What is the matter?"

"It's not the right size," Rebecca argued. "She made it too thick; it needs to be thinner on the side for it to look right."

Meghan cocked her head to the side. "I disagree," she said to her mother. Meghan saw Pamela's upset face, and she put a shoulder around the girl. "Pamela, you are doing a great job. Keep it up."

Rebecca frowned. "No, Pamela," she insisted. "You aren't doing it correctly."

Meghan stepped in front of her mother and shook her head. "That's enough, Mama," she told Rebecca. "We may be doing your recipe, but this is my bakery. We do things a certain way here, and if I say Pamela's braid looks nice, then that's the way it is."

Rebecca's jaw dropped, but she quickly regained composure and straightened her posture. "Fine," she huffed to Meghan. "I'll just be quiet and go work on the icing."

After awhile, Rebecca's mood softened, and she and

Trudy chatted about their favorite treats to bake. "My favorite holiday treats are egg-nog eclairs," Trudy told Rebecca. "They have such a unique, festive flavor."

"Those sound delightful," Rebecca affirmed as she dropped four drops of red food coloring into the bowl of frothy icing. "My favorite treat to bake is a coconut custard tart topped with roasted pineapple."

Meghan gasped. "That sounds incredible, Mama," she gushed as Rebecca's eyes sparkled.

"It's your father's favorite," Rebecca declared. "Many Christmases ago, my family attended a party at your father's parents' house. I whipped up one of my coconut tarts, but as I tasted it, I felt it needed more flavor. I looked around my Mama's kitchen, and when I saw a fresh pineapple, I knew it would be the perfect touch for my treat. I roasted the pineapple and cut the pieces into little stars in honor of the holiday."

Meghan's heart warmed at the dreamy look on her mother's face. "Then what happened?"

"I took the dessert to the party, and when your father tried it, he demanded to be introduced to the baker. I was the baker! We were introduced, and it was love at first bite, as we like to say."

Meghan's face glowed as she imagined her parents as young people in Texas. "That's the best story, Mama. I've never heard it before!"

Rebecca nodded. "It just goes to show that food is a

way to a man's heart. In fact, we should finish up these treats and take some to Jack at the station. Didn't you tell me he worked a double shift?"

Meghan bit her lip. "He did," she confirmed. "He's been working day and night to find out just how Roger died."

"Then it's settled," Rebecca announced. "We will finish these treats and then take some to Jack. I have an idea! How about we recreate some of the holiday magic I shared with your father years ago?"

Meghan nervously raised an eyebrow. "What do you mean?"

Rebecca gave her daughter a sly look. "We have all of the ingredients we need here," she said. "What if we made coconut tarts with roasted pineapples on top? That was the key to your father's heart, and I'm sure Jack would be delighted to share in some of our family fun! Come on, Meghan! Say yes. It did wonders for your father and me; those tarts are the whole reason you are here."

Meghan giggled. "Well, I don't think the tarts are the only reason I'm here, Mama…"

"Oh, you silly girl. Come on, my dear. Indulge me. Roll up your sleeves, and let's make some of the tarts for your man. It'll make magic happen for you two, I guarantee it!"

Thirty minutes later, Meghan bid farewell to Pamela and Trudy as they left the bakery. She and Rebecca packed up the warm tarts, and they bundled up in their heavy coats to brave the cold night air. It was a windy night, and the breeze stung Meghan's cheeks. "Are you sure you don't want to buy a second home in the Bahamas?" Meghan joked to Rebecca as she navigated through a snow bank.

"Don't tempt me," her Mum countered.

The two arrived at the Sandy Bay Police Station and were directed to Jack's office. As they walked down the hallway, they heard the booming voice of Roberto Luciano. "I had nothing to do with that man's demise," Roberto insisted as he stormed down the hallway past Meghan and Rebecca, Chief Nunan trailing behind him with a notebook in her hands. "This incident is ruining my business. We had ten cancellations last night for our dinner hours, and today, fifteen people have cancelled! I am going to have to close down my restaurant if something doesn't change. This is preposterous!"

Meghan cringed as Roberto began shouting in Italian. "He is so angry," she whispered to her mother as they watched him stalk down the hallway.

"He has a right to be," Rebecca said. "That man dropping dead in front of his restaurant isn't good for business, just as he said. It's quite sad that such a fine restaurant is losing patrons."

Meghan shrugged. "I think it's quite sad that a man passed away, and all anyone seems to care about is business. Between Roberto and Kayley, it seems like people don't care that a poor man who was down on his luck is now gone. Where is the holiday spirit?"

"I see plenty of the holiday spirit right here."

Meghan looked up to see Jack grinning down at her. He looked tired; with the deep, heavy bags beneath his eyes, his disheveled clothes, and his matted hair, it was evident that he had been working nonstop.

"How are the two most beautiful ladies in Sandy Bay?" Jack asked Meghan and Rebecca.

"We're just fine, Jack," Rebecca answered. "We brought something to you. Meghan says you've been working around the clock, and we thought you needed a treat. Now, I'm sure you wouldn't have to work such long hours if you had a nice, proper business job, but we'll let that be."

Jack gritted his teeth and pasted a smile on his face. "Thank you for thinking of me," he said to Rebecca. "What kind of treat?"

Meghan held up a white wicker basket. "It's filled with coconut tarts topped with roasted pineapple," she said to Jack. "We baked them fresh this afternoon. I was telling Meghan that these were the first treats I ever made for her father, and that you would adore the surprise as well. We're keeping a dear family tradition alive!"

Jack beamed. "You are too good to me," he murmured to Meghan as he lifted a tart out of the basket and took a bite. "This is delicious. Meghan, you are such a sweetheart. I'm going to get you anything you want for Christmas. Anything!"

Rebecca glanced up at Meghan and winked. "See?" she whispered to Meghan. "Food is the key to a man's heart. Maybe by next Christmas, there will be something special on your finger, Meghan. You heard the guy; he's going to get you anything you want for Christmas."

10

THE SANDY BAY FOOD BANK was held each morning at the Sandy Bay Community Gymnasium. Meghan was shocked by how many people were present; by her count, nearly two-hundred homeless people were in line for food and services, and she smiled as she watched groups of people happily eat their meals.

"This is quite the production," Rebecca remarked to Angela as she led them through the gym. "What an efficient process."

"It's great, isn't it?" Angela replied as she walked in front of Rebecca and Meghan. "One of my dear friends from college runs a major food bank on the East Coast, and every year, she comes out here to help us improve our system. Here, come around to the serving side. I'll show you how it's done."

Meghan watched in awe as Angela joined a group of servers giving food to a line of homeless men. The process was efficient; every server gave exactly the same amount of food to each guest, and the portions were very generous. The meals consisted of chicken, spinach salad, an orange, and a roasted red pepper, and Meghan was impressed by the quality of the food. "The servers all give out food in unison," she said in amazement. "How do they do it?"

Angela stepped forward and joined the line, grabbing a serving spoon and smiling at the guest in front of her while still speaking to Meghan. "We offer a half-day training for everyone who wants to help," she told Meghan as she scooped up a serving of chicken and placed it on a tray. "We train our volunteers to serve quickly and fairly; everyone gets a large, healthy meal, and everyone can leave here with full bellies and good service."

Meghan watched as Angela served three guests in a row in under ten seconds. "You are so fast."

"It's the training," Angela told her. "We practice serving and use timers, and we bring in treats and prizes to make it more like a competition. It's all great fun, and we have a steady group here. I've been volunteering here for years, so I know our guests pretty well."

"It's sweet that you call them guests," Rebecca said as she eyed a man in a tattered pair of overalls.

Angela shrugged. "Here, these folks are our guests. Homeless people matter. They have feelings and needs. We don't believe that if someone is down on their luck, that their life loses value. Sure, it gets frustrating when these people gather in front of our restaurant and scare away customers, but at the end of the day, they are just people."

Meghan looked around the crowded gym. "What can we do to help?" she asked Angela.

"You haven't been trained in the serving process, but you could go chat with some of our guests," Angela told Meghan. "There's a spot at that table over there. Rebecca? Why don't you go visit the nursery? We offer childcare during meal times, and you might enjoy visiting with the little kids."

Meghan and Rebecca set off in their different directions. Meghan took a seat at a table of middle-aged men. "Hi," she said to the man beside her. "I'm Meghan. What's your name?"

The man was dressed in a ratty sock cap and a dirty turtleneck. He had a thick beard that curled around his collarbone, and Meghan could smell his greasy hair. "Why are you talking to me?"

Meghan smiled. "I'm visiting today," she said to the man. "I might start volunteering here."

The man laughed. "Oh, a little spoiled princess working with the poor? That's rich."

A woman beside him elbowed the man in the side. "Alan, be nice to her. She's just being friendly."

Alan frowned. "It's embarrassing that rich folks come in here and talk with us poor people," he replied briskly to the woman. "Look at this girl. She looks like she ain't ever done a lick of hard work in her life."

Meghan pursed her lips and nervously played with her hands beneath the table. "I have worked before," she insisted. "I work at a bakery in town. I own it, actually."

Alan narrowed his eyes and stared into Meghan's face. "Oh? How much of your food do you donate to us homeless? Judging from the look on your face, I would guess that you don't give anything away. I hate that. I hate when rich little girls march in here to volunteer for the day, but in reality, they don't really care. If you really care, little rich girl, you would donate food from your bakery to feed the poor."

"You are right," Meghan agreed. "I should do that. I don't know why I never thought of it, but that is something I need to start doing."

Alan rolled his eyes. "Don't talk down to me, rich girl," he growled as he balled his hands into fists. "You need to get out of my face."

Meghan shook her head. "I just wanted to come over and say hi," she pleaded with the man as his face darkened. "I'm sorry if I offended you."

Alan glared at Meghan and rose to his feet. "Little rich girl here is sorry she offended me, huh? You don't want to know what happened to the last fellow who offended me, rich girl."

Meghan's eyes widened as Alan stormed away. "Just ignore him," the woman begged Meghan. "He doesn't mean to be bad, and we are truly grateful for the chance to get meals here."

Meghan nodded. "It's okay," she said to the woman as she pulled her dark hair back into a ponytail. "I feel bad that I offended him."

Alan circled back around to the table and resumed sitting by Meghan. "Sorry," he muttered as Meghan leaned away from him. "I get angry sometimes. Sorry I was nasty."

Meghan forced herself to smile. "It's fine," she said. "I just want to visit with everyone and spread some holiday cheer."

"I had enough holiday cheer this year," Alan laughed as Meghan raised an eyebrow. "That loser Roger Williams died. That brought enough cheer to my heart for the year."

Meghan's mouth dropped open. "Did you know him?"

Alan smirked. "Oh, I knew him. That idiot didn't deserve to become the store Santa, and I'm glad he...dropped dead before he could."

Alan turned around and grabbed a loaf of bread from the table behind him. "I'm extra hungry today," he said as he stuffed the bread into his mouth.

 The table behind him yelled. "That's ours," they shouted. "You jerk."

Alan rose to his feet and grimaced as a portly man from the other table walked over and shoved him. Alan kicked the man's knees, and the man fell to the ground. Alan chuckled to himself as everyone stared at him.

"You all had better let me do what I want," he yelled to the crowd of shocked bystanders. "I wanted more bread, so I took it. I wanted to be the Santa at the store, so....just listen up, people. You mess with me, and I'll mess with you. You should see the last guy I messed with. He was *dying* to get away from me."

A collective gasped filled the room, and Alan's eyes bulged out from his head. "I didn't kill Roger, or did I? I know what you all are thinking. I'm out of here."

Meghan stared as Alan turned on his heel and bolted out of the gym. She reached into her red purse and retrieved her cell phone, quickly dialing Jack's number. "Babe," she breathed into the phone as Jack answered. "I think I know who did it. I think I know who murdered Roger."

11

"I'M JUST NOT SURE, Meghan," Jack said as the pair talked on the phone later in the evening. "The officers brought him in and talked with him, but I'm just not sure if this is our guy."

Meghan snuggled deeper into her bed and pulled the comforter up to her neck. She could see the snow falling out the window, and she felt cozy and comfortable amidst the three chai-scented candles burning in her bedroom. Fiesta and Siesta were asleep at her feet, and Meghan wiggled her toes beneath their warm little bodies.

"You *did* say that Alan had a checkered past," Meghan replied to her boyfriend. "You told me that Chief Nunan pulled some records of his. I even read online that there's even an arrest warrant out for him right now. He stole some cans of tomatoes from the store last week!"

Jack sighed into the phone, and Meghan could hear the angst as he replied. "He kept saying he was innocent, Meghan. You should have heard him; he sounded so earnest as he pleaded with Chief Nunan."

Meghan remembered how intimidated she had been when Alan taunted her at the food bank. He had scared her, and Meghan sensed that Alan was not just an ordinary homeless man. He struck her as a killer, and Meghan's gut was telling her that something was amiss.

"I know he scared you," Jack said. "Don't worry, he's being held in jail pending further investigation into the murder case. Chief Nunan mentioned that there was a similar case to this one out in Maine, and perhaps we have a serial killer on our hands. She wants us to be thoroughly cautious, so she's confined Alan to an isolated cell until we can learn more."

Meghan sighed in relief. "That's good to hear," she told him. "He was so frightening, Jack. He had a scary look in his eyes."

Jack's voice broke. "I just don't want to mess this case up," he choked as Meghan's heart began to race.

"Jack?" Meghan asked in concern. "What's wrong? What's the matter?"

Jack cleared his throat. "It's nothing. I just have some things on my mind."

Meghan bit her lip. "I'm here if you need me, Jack," she said. "I love you."

"I love you too, Meghan," Jack replied, and Meghan's heart soared with those three special words. "I just don't think he did it. My gut is telling me that he didn't. What does Alan have to gain?"

Meghan raised her eyebrows. "The prize money," she argued. "He could have wanted to be the Santa at the store, and Roger was going to be given the part. What if Alan wanted the prize money?"

"That's what Chief Nunan said," Jack admitted. "But I don't know. My gut is telling me something else. Listen, I'm going to get off the phone and go for a walk. I need to clear my head."

"Okay, bye, love," Meghan said as she hung up the phone.

Meghan's cell phone immediately buzzed. Thinking it was Jack, she answered without pausing. She was surprised to hear her father's voice.

"Meghan, what are you up to?"

She looked around her bedroom. "I'm all snuggled up for the night," she said to her father. "Why, Daddy?"

"The snow is falling like crazy, and the moon is so bright. I'm dying to get out of this hotel room. Let's go for a nighttime walk. What do you say?"

Meghan groaned, but she knew that she needed to spend as much time as possible with her parents before they left. "Of course, Daddy," she answered. "Let's meet at the beach in twenty minutes. I'll bring the dogs; they look so precious in their winter coats, and they can't wait to see their Grandpa."

It was nine in the evening by the time Meghan and Henry made it to the beach, but the light of the moon lit up the sand and the sky. "It's just beautiful," Henry gushed as he guided Fiesta along the shore. "The snow looks like diamonds! Your mother would sure like it."

Meghan giggled. "Mama loves diamonds, but she hates getting cold," she replied. "I think she's in the perfect spot in her hotel room, that's for sure."

Henry chuckled good-naturedly, and then, he pointed to a lone figure in the distance. "Hey, isn't that your man, Meghan? That's Jack. Look! He has a dog with him."

Meghan whistled, and Dash, Jack's dog, sprinted toward her. Jack ran after the dog, and he smiled when he realized it was Meghan who had called for Dash. "Meghan. Henry. What a surprise."

Meghan leapt into Jack's arms. "I didn't know you would come here to walk. I'm so happy to see you. Are you doing better, babe?"

Jack looked down at his boots, and Henry playfully nudged Jack on the shoulder. "What's wrong, son? Rough day at the office?"

Jack hesitated. "I shouldn't say…"

"Oh, come on, sport," Henry argued. "Tell us what's the matter. My little girl shouldn't have to worry about her man. What's the issue?"

Jack sighed. "It's about the man we arrested. Alan? The homeless man? I just don't think he did it, and I feel terrible."

Meghan placed a hand on Jack's shoulder. "I've never seen you so upset about a case before," she murmured. "Is there something standing out to you about this man?"

Jack's shoulders shook, and Meghan could see that he was trying not to cry. "I just feel like my gut is telling me he is innocent, and I would hate to keep an innocent man locked up. I kept an innocent man locked up for two whole weeks during my rookie year, and man, I never forgot the look on his daughter's face when he was released. I was just doing my job, but she looked at me as if I had hurt someone."

Henry placed a hand on Jack's shoulder and squeezed. "Sport, you can't be too hard on yourself," he said. "If you are following the rules and the law, you are doing what society expects of you. You can't give up, Jack. I'm sure it's difficult, but you have to do your job."

Jack frowned. "It's just hard to ignore my gut."

Henry shrugged. "In life, we have to do hard things," he told him. "In my business, I've had to fire people, and to make hard decisions. The beauty of it is that from hard choices come better outcomes, and I know that if you work hard and do your job, things will work out."

Jack smiled weakly. "Thanks, Mr. Truman," he said.

Henry furrowed his brow. "Really, call me Henry," he insisted.

Meghan's eyes sparkled as she watched the two most important men in her life share a moment together. Her heart warmed, and she felt a sense of relief as Henry embraced her boyfriend.

"Mama is warming to Jack," she thought to herself. "And Daddy is warming to him. Maybe this whole thing--Sandy Bay, the bakery, and Jack--will work out after all."

12

"I'M SO GLAD WE COULD GET TOGETHER and do this," Kayley Kane schmoozed as she led Rebecca and Meghan down the street toward a potential property. "You two have been such good sports with this snow and cold weather. Don't worry, though; this is our last place for the day."

Kayley held out her arms to show Rebecca and Meghan a four-story vacant building right beside Luciano's. "It's been empty for awhile, but it could be the perfect place for a shop, or a restaurant, or even a combination."

Rebecca raised an eyebrow. "It looks a little...rough, Ms. Kane."

Kayley sighed. "It was previously used to house some of the homeless," she admitted to Rebecca. "The owner of the building is moving to the East Coast and wants to sell it quickly, but he wants to sell it to someone with the right priorities."

"What do you mean by that?" Meghan asked as Kayley tapped her heeled shoes against the sidewalk.

Kayley chewed on her bottom lip before responding. "Well, Roberto Luciano tried to buy this place," she explained to the Trumans. "It *is* just next door to his place. But the owner didn't think Luciano had the right priorities. The owner of the property wants someone with empathy toward the homeless to purchase it, and he didn't feel like Roberto showed that. Roberto's been known for screaming and shouting at the homeless people, and the owner didn't feel right about leaving the property with him."

Rebecca frowned. "If that is the standard--empathy toward the homeless--I don't know if I would make the cut," she told Kayley. "I feel for them, I do, but I would not use this property to better them. I would likely turn it into something fabulous--this town *needs* a designer handbag shop--and I wouldn't prioritize the homeless' needs while arranging my next business endeavor."

Kayley smiled weakly at Rebecca. "Are you sure? You didn't warm to any of the other properties. Are you sure you couldn't just donate some money to the homeless, or perhaps work with a local agency to employ a homeless person in the store?"

Rebecca frowned. "I believe I made myself clear," she told Kayley. "None of the properties you have shown me have blown me away, Ms. Kane. Until something marvelous comes along, I'm afraid I cannot make a sale with you."

Meghan saw the look of concern in Kayley's eyes. "Mama, why don't you think about some of the places from earlier? That first little building was cute;

you could turn that into a little salon or boutique."

Rebecca sighed. "You are so soft, Meghan," she hissed. "I want the best, and Kayley hasn't shown me the best."

Kayley sputtered, knowing that she had possibly blown the sale. "I will make a list of alternative properties," she announced to the Trumans. "Just you wait, ladies. I will come up with the finest places in Sandy Bay, and Mrs. Truman, I can assure you that you will be pleasantly surprised."

"I sure hope so," Rebecca sniffed. "Kayley, I think that's enough for us today. Meghan? Let's go."

Meghan and Rebecca said goodbye to Kayley and walked away. "I just don't know what she was thinking," Rebecca complained. "The properties were fine, but that last one? The stipulations on it were too much. I'm happy to spend a day at a food bank, and Daddy and I write a personal check each year to the shelter in town. I just don't believe mixing business and handouts. It seems wrong to me."

Meghan pursed her lips. "I don't think it's too much to ask for, Mama," she told Rebecca. "It sounds like the only requirement is simply to respect the homeless and to provide some sort of opportunity for them. Is that too much?"

Rebecca rolled her eyes. "Meghan, if I am going to buy a second home here and open a little business for fun, it's going to be on my terms. Besides, Daddy would never approve of hiring a homeless person to work in a store of ours, and his opinion matters, too."

Meghan walked silently beside her mother, aghast at how privileged and selfish her mother could be. Meghan knew that Rebecca lived in a world of wealth and finery, but she wished that her mother could step outside of herself and see the needs of those around her. From Kayley's desire and need to make a sale with the Trumans, to the homeless, Rebecca seemed oblivious to the plights of those less fortunate than herself.

"Why are you making that sour face?" Rebecca asked her daughter. "Really, you should watch the way you hold your face, Meghan; it could freeze like that if you are not careful, or you could get wrinkles."

Meghan gritted her teeth. "Mama, I think there are more important matters at stake than my face," she huffed. "Kayley really needs to make a sale with you and Daddy. She is a single mom, and her ex-husband hardly helps with anything."

Rebecca narrowed her eyes. "Her finances are not my concern," she explained to her daughter. "Nor are they yours. She should not have mentioned her ex-husband, or her son's schooling. That was very unprofessional, and if she worked anywhere other than this tiny town, she would be fired for that kind of rude behavior."

Meghan sighed. "Mama, Sandy Bay is different than the South," she argued. "All of the prim and proper rules don't matter here. In Sandy Bay, people are candid. They speak their minds here, and they say what they mean. Kayley is worried about making ends meet, and I know how much it would help her to receive a large commission from a sale with you and Daddy."

Rebecca shook her head. "Really, Meghan, you should hear yourself. It's disgraceful. Talking about a stranger's finances is unacceptable."

Meghan crossed her arms in front of her chest. "No, Mama," she responded. "Not caring is unacceptable. We have so much, Mama, and we should be happy to share with others. We've been so blessed and comfortable, and our family should be honored to help others get by."

Rebecca glared at her daughter. "I don't know what's gotten into you," she said to Meghan. "But this behavior is unseemly. This is not a conversation I care to have anymore, so I must excuse myself. I am going back to the hotel and going to the gym."

"The gym?" Meghan asked.

"Yes," Rebecca answered. "I've been indulging during this trip. I typically only eat greens and tofu, but being around the bakery has awoken my sweet tooth. I need to work off some of this nastiness on the elliptical as soon as possible."

Meghan smiled. "I have an idea," she told her mother, eager to salvage their day together. "Remember my friend, Karen Denton? She is the queen of exercise. She always knows the hippest, trendiest places to squeeze in a sweat. How about I give her a call? We can work out together?"

Rebecca's face brightened. "You are suggesting we work out? How wonderful! I never thought those words would come out of your mouth, but I am so thrilled they did. Give Karen a call. Tell her we will meet her in an hour, and beforehand, I'll take you to Spark to buy a cute workout outfit. How do you feel about spandex?"

13

MEGHAN STARED AT HER REFLECTION in the mirror of Karen's guest bathroom. She hardly recognized herself in the workout outfit her mother had purchased for her; the tight, clingy leggings and the matching pale pink sweatshirt were not items she would have chosen for herself, but as she studied her appearance, Meghan was pleasantly surprised at how the bottoms accentuated her curves. The leggings were snug in the bottom, and Meghan turned around to admire her backside. "I don't look half bad in nice workout clothes," Meghan admitted as she adjusted the crew neck sweatshirt. "Maybe with the right outfit, I'll enjoy working out more."

Meghan was wrong; despite her expensive new clothes, she detested exercise, and as she ran alongside her mother and Karen, she struggled to catch her breath.

"Try to keep up, Meghan," Rebecca chided her daughter as the women jogged along the main street of Sandy Bay. "We're going at a pace that is ridiculously slow for Karen and me. Surely you can move your legs faster?"

Meghan frowned, but she did her best to pick up her legs at a faster speed. "I'm coming," she called out.

"You're doing a fabulous job, Sweetie," Karen complimented as Meghan caught up to her. "I'm so proud of you."

Meghan smiled, thankful that someone was recognizing her hard work. "I'm doing my best," she grunted.

Rebecca quickened the pace, moving gracefully in a pair of soft periwinkle leggings and a matching knee-length workout sweater. "Come on, ladies, let's step it up," Rebecca ordered. "My trainer back home is going to kick my booty if he finds out I ate my weight in holiday treats here in Sandy Bay. Let's burn some el-bees, girls!"

Rebecca took off at a sprint. Karen followed, and Meghan attempted to keep up. "What are they doing?" Meghan wondered to herself as Rebecca and Karen quickly decreased their speed.

"We're doing intervals," Karen informed Meghan with a grin. "We run fast for thirty seconds, and then, we slow our pace. It's so good for your heart, and it's the best way to burn fat."

Rebecca nodded as she jogged beside her daughter. "Come on, Meghan. Burn some fat with us. It'll be the best gift you give yourself this Christmas."

Before Meghan could respond, Rebecca and Karen took off in a sprint again. "Come on, Meghan," Karen yelled. "It's only thirty seconds of hard work! You can do it."

Meghan took a deep breath. She picked up her knees and pumped her arms vigorously, but just as she reached her fastest pace, her mother and Karen slowed down. Meghan could feel the frustration fill her heart, and she struggled to stay positive as her athletic mother and friend raced down the street. The three women sprinted and jogged for a half hour, and finally, it was time for them to cool down.

"We'll just do a little two mile run to cool down," Karen said as she high-fived Rebecca. "Feeling good, Meghan?"

Meghan nodded. "I'm....feeling something," she responded breathlessly.

Karen smiled at Meghan. "So, how is Jack doing, Sweetie? I haven't seen much of him in town, lately."

Meghan sighed. "He's been so busy with the case," she told Karen. "I've barely seen him myself."

Karen nodded. "Who do you think did it, Meghan? Does Jack know of any leads?"

Rebecca interjected. "My husband told me that Jack doesn't think that other homeless man, Alan, killed Roger," she said to Karen. "He says that Jack told him that he believes Alan is innocent. I have to disagree. I saw the way that terrible Alan upset my daughter at the food bank, and I think he had something to do with it."

Meghan agreed. "I didn't feel safe around him," she confirmed. "He was a big man, and he had a terrifying look in his eyes. He even told the crowd that he had messed with people before, and I think he meant that he killed Roger."

Karen slowed the pace. "We're going too fast for a cool down, ladies," she warned Rebecca and Meghan. "Anyway, that's terrible that Alan scared you, Meghan. Any other thoughts? They don't have any other suspects, do they?"

Meghan bobbed her head. "Actually, they do have another official suspect," she told Karen. "Roberto Luciano?"

Karen gasped. "Robbie? They think Robbie Luciano killed that man? There's no way he did that."

Meghan shivered as a gust of cold air hit her face. "From what I heard, they think he could have killed Roger because of his disdain for the homeless. A group of homeless guys hangs out outside of Roberto's restaurant nearly every night, and Roberto feels like he loses business because of it."

Karen shook her head. "I just cannot imagine Robbie Luciano hurting a fly," she insisted. "He and his family are such wonderful additions to the community. His wife, Maria, volunteers at the library each morning. His son, Francisco, donated a kidney to a little boy in town who needed a donor. His daughter, Angela, is one of the main coordinators for the local food bank. I just don't believe anyone in that family could have anything to do with the death; the

Lucianos just don't have a mean bone in their bodies."

Meghan agreed. "That's how I feel as well," she told Karen. "Roberto gets frustrated with the homeless, but I don't think he is a killer."

Rebecca frowned. "If I were in his situation, though, I would sure be angry," she told the women. "If I owned a fine restaurant in the middle of town, and a group of rowdy homeless men were constantly around, I would be furious. I'm already furious that my own daughter has to deal with such scoundrels in her own town. I hope Roberto didn't kill that man, but if he did, I would understand. What a nuisance."

Meghan's jaw dropped at her mother's callous words. "Mother, how can you say something like that?"

Rebecca maintained her pace. "Obviously I don't condone murder, Meghan; don't be daft. I'm just saying that it's frustrating to see so many people like Roger in one town."

"What do you mean, 'like Roger?'" Meghan asked her mother. "You mean, homeless? Poor? Down on their luck?"

"Precisely," Rebecca answered. "It's terrible to see so many of those people in the place where my daughter lives. I don't think a nice man like Roberto Luciano would kill a homeless man, but if he did, I would surely empathize with his frustrations."

Meghan tugged at the sweatshirt; it was tight around

her neck, and her mother's brash words shocked her, making her throat feel tight and her chest swollen in disappointment. "Mama, do you know what holiday is coming up?"

Rebecca smirked. "Of course. It's almost Christmas."

Meghan nodded. "Exactly. And Christmas is all about love, the birth of Jesus in a manger and taking care of those less fortunate than us. I can hardly believe a loving, good woman such as yourself could empathize with someone for killing, but not with the homeless and downtrodden. It shocks me, Mama."

Rebecca came to an abrupt halt. "That is not what I meant, Meghan Truman," she insisted. "You know that. Don't make me out to be some kind of cruel monster."

Karen stepped between the mother and daughter. "Let's change the subject," she said. "What if there is someone we haven't thought of who could be the killer? Wouldn't it be funny if Sally Sheridan had killed him?"

Meghan's eyes widened. "Karen! That's a terrible thing to say."

Karen giggled. "I'm only joking," she said. "But seriously, if Sally Sheridan killed that man, she'd probably get caught trying to get a refund on his body! She would take it back to the coroner to see if she could get some money back."

Meghan erupted into laughter. It had been a tense

afternoon with her mother, and despite the macabre nature of Karen's joke, Meghan was thankful for her dear friend for clearing the air. "You are too much, Karen Denton," Meghan said. "You are too much."

Rebecca huffed, reaching down to loosen the string on her pants. "I think I need to go shopping," she said as she let out a sigh of relief. "This run was nice, but I don't think it solved my problems. Meghan, your father and I have a party to attend just hours after we arrive home in Texas, and I am in need of some new dress pants. How about we take a little jog over to the department store in town? Karen, would you like to join us?"

Karen clapped her hands. "I'm always up for a little jog," she told Rebecca. "Even if it is to a department store."

14

AS MEGHAN, KAREN, AND REBECCA WALKED into Sandy Bay Station, the biggest department store in town, Meghan's stomach churned as she realized the racks were nearly bare. "Mama is not going to be happy," she thought to herself. "And I'm sure she'll let us all know that."

Rebecca darted from one section to the next, picking up articles of clothing, wrinkling her nose, and dismissing her finds. "I don't understand," she declared. "How can this department store have enough money to fund a $25,000 prize for an amateur actor to play Santa Clause, but *this* is the state of the store?"

Karen nodded. "I haven't been in here in a few months," she admitted. "But the inventory is just sad. I wonder what happened here."

Meghan perused a shabby holiday display, cringing at the static playing over the in-store radio. "I don't know if we're going to find what you're looking for, Mama," she whispered to Rebecca. "It seems like slim-pickings here. Why don't we try Spark? They have some cute things, and I'm sure we could find something for you. Or we could drive up to Portland. I'm sure they have some designer stores there."

Rebecca shook her head. "Let's just keep looking," she told her daughter. "Why don't you ask an associate if there is more merchandise upstairs? Maybe they've hidden some things away."

Meghan scurried away to the Help Desk and found a sales associate. He was tall and thin, with pasty skin and thick glasses. Meghan flashed her brightest smile and waved. "Hi! I'm Meghan. I'm looking for outfits for women in their mid-fifties. Do you have other sections with things like that?"

The boy shuffled awkwardly behind the desk. "This is all we have, Ma'am."

Meghan cocked her head to the side. "Really? This is the largest store in town. You guys sponsor that major Christmas competition each year for the homeless. What kind of major store has almost no inventory?"

The boy shrugged. "This is just between us," he whispered, leaning in toward Meghan. "The store is under some major pressure from Corporate, and from what my manager told me, we might be going under."

Meghan's eyes widened. "Seriously?"

"Yeah," the boy nodded. "It's awful; I've worked here for two years, and when you make it to your third year, you get a big bonus. If we close before next October, I won't get my bonus, and I'll have no job."

"That's terrible," she said. "Do you think things will get better?"

The boy shook his head. "Rumor around the staff lounge is that cuts are going to be made soon. Those at the bottom of the seniority list will be let go, and then, they'll start working down from the top. It's a mess."

Meghan gave him a sympathetic look. "I'm sorry to hear that. Business can be so complicated."

The boy raised an eyebrow. "You know, you look familiar. I've seen you before. Aren't you Meghan Truman, the owner of that little bakery?"

Meghan smiled. "Guilty as charged."

"Are you hiring by any chance?" whispered the boy as Meghan bit her lip. "A few buddies from the store and I could really use something more stable. Any way you would take on some extra hands in the New Year?"

Meghan pursed her lips. "I'm not sure about that," she admitted. "Things are very stable at my bakery, and I don't know how I could budget for additional staff. I'll keep you in my thoughts, though. I'm sorry things are tense here at the store."

The boy gave Meghan a weak smile. "Thanks," he said. "And by the way, there's rack of nice clothes for women upstairs. It's the last of our women's inventory, and we just set it out today. You had better make your way up there before someone else gets to it."

"Thanks," Meghan said. "And happy holidays."

An hour later, the three ladies were sipping on coffee at Bean, the coffee shop around the corner from the bakery. Meghan was friendly with the owner, and he always gave her a discount on her lattes.

"I think it's cute," Karen argued with Rebecca over the outfit she had chosen. "It's not designer, and it's not fancy, but I think the lilac will be such a pretty color on you."

"Yes, it will," Meghan agreed. "Mama, everything doesn't always have to be fancy, and I think it's good you made a purchase. The sales associate told me the store is struggling, and I'm glad we could help."

Rebecca rolled her eyes. "Meghan, what have I told you? You cannot get invested in the business of salespeople. If the store is struggling, that isn't our problem. I just hope this lilac suit will be worth the thirty dollars I paid for it."

"At least it was a bargain," Meghan offered as Rebecca scoffed.

"Hey, what's that on the news?" Karen asked, pointing at the little television in the corner of the coffee shop. "That looks like the department store."

"Let me go turn it up," Meghan replied. She walked to the television and turned up the volume. A gaggle of employees from the store were being featured, and

Meghan spotted the sales associate who had helped her. The screen then flashed back to a red-haired reporter holding a green microphone.

"Breaking news from our local department store," the reporter stated as she grimly read from the offscreen teleprompter. "Christian Evans, the managing director of the store, is under investigation for fraudulent activities. He is also reported to have embezzled over a quarter of a million dollars from the store's employee compensation account."

"Mama, did you hear that?" Meghan asked as she stared at the screen. "That explains why the racks were so bare."

"In a statement from the Corporate office in Indianapolis, Indiana, it appears that if the allegations are true, the Sandy Bay location will be shut down immediately."

The shot flashed to a suited woman with glasses shaking her head at the camera. "I'm Miranda Mullins, the CEO, and it is a shame that this is happening in one of our stores," she lamented. "This has jeopardized the health of our company. From my records, it appears we wouldn't have even been able to sponsor the $25,000 Santa Clause competition in Sandy Bay given our finances. What a shame."

Meghan's jaw dropped. She turned the volume back down on the television and returned to her seat. "Can you believe that?" she asked her mother and Karen. "That Christian Evans stole all of that money, and now, his people will be out of jobs."

Karen shook her head. "Christian has always been a greedy scoundrel," she informed the group. "I grew up with him; he's a Sandy Bay local, but he doesn't have a Sandy Bay heart. He used to steal money from our school charities when we were children, and I heard that when he divorced his wife, he left her with nothing. No, I can't say I'm surprised he's behind something like this."

Rebecca clucked. "He is innocent until proven guilty," she haughtily told Karen. "We shouldn't jump to conclusions."

Meghan frowned. "I think it's a pretty clear conclusion," she said slowly. "The man who was set to win the $25,000 prize dies out of the blue, and then it comes out that there was going to be no prize and the department store is going under? It sounds fishy to me."

Karen's lips turned downward into a frown. "Meghan, do you think Jack knows anything about this? I think Christian Evans is the perfect suspect; he has the motive and the means, and I wouldn't be shocked if he killed that fellow with his own two greedy hands."

Meghan whipped out her cell phone and began dialing. "I think you're right," she agreed. "I'm giving Jack a call right now."

Jack picked up on the first ring. "Sweetheart?"

"Jack, have you seen the news?" Meghan asked. "That Christian Evans guy? The manager at the department store? I think he has a serious reason to have done away with the man who died."

Jack groaned. "Ugh, I was hoping that news wouldn't be broken so quickly," he admitted. "I didn't want it to turn into a field day at the department store. Don't worry, babe; we have our team investigating Mr. Evans. We've been watching him for weeks."

Meghan smiled, relieved that Jack knew of her concerns. "You're always on the case, Jack," she gushed. "You're always on top of things."

15

IT WAS A TRULY FESTIVE EVENING at the bakery. Meghan had ordered three boxes of holiday decorations from Spark, and as Jack and Pamela helped her dress up Truly Sweet, Christmas music played in the background. Meghan had made a plate of fresh, steaming cinnamon rolls for the occasion, and as she hung ornaments and strung lights, her heart was filled with joy.

"This is my favorite time of the year," Pamela exclaimed as she wound a strand of garland around the front counter. "It's just magical!"

"I agree," Jack replied as he took a sip of the coffee Meghan had made for him. He was still working double shifts, and she was thrilled that he was able to steal away for a few hours to help her decorate.

Meghan smiled as she reached into the last of the three boxes from Spark. "Oooh, look at these," she said to Pamela and Jack. "A set of jingle bells! They are so shiny and beautiful. The designs on each bell are just spectacular."

Pamela dropped the strand of garland and ran to

Meghan's side. "Wow," she murmured in appreciation as she examined the jingle bells. "They are gorgeous, Meghan. Can I hang them up somewhere special?"

"Of course," she answered. "Jingle bells bring good luck! Why don't you hang them on the register, Pamela? Maybe they'll bring good luck to my business."

Pamela laughed at Meghan's joke. "This place looks so pretty. Thanks for inviting me to help you deck the halls."

Suddenly, Meghan heard the familiar tone of Jack's work phone. She groaned, disappointed that her beloved boyfriend would likely be called to the station sooner than later.

"This is Detective Irvin," Jack answered in a business-like tone. "Yes, Chief, I am available."

Meghan's heart sank. She had been having such an enjoyable evening, and now, Jack would have to leave. He had been so busy with work lately, and she felt as though they had hardly gotten to do any fun, festive holiday activities. She tried to keep a pleasant look on her face as Jack hung up the phone and walked to her, but Meghan felt the frown creep across her lips.

"What's wrong?" Jack asked.

"Nothing," Meghan responded. "I'm just sad that you have to leave. That was Chief Nunan, I heard. Do you have to go?"

Jack nodded. "I'm sorry," he said. "It's for work. Surely you understand."

Meghan bit her lip. "I've just had to understand a lot, lately," she said sharply. "You've been working so much."

Jack thought for a moment. "I have an idea," he said. "Chief Nunan said they'll only need me for an hour or so. How about you send Pamela home, and then you can ride with me to the station? We can go out for a drink or a treat after. What do you say?"

Meghan paused, but seeing the hopeful look in Jack's eyes, she smiled. "That sounds fine," she told him.

When Jack and Meghan arrived at the station twenty minutes later, Chief Nunan met them at the door. "It's a big break, Jack," she told him as they walked down the hall toward the interrogation room. "He told us he is ready to confess, but for some reason, he wanted you in attendance."

Meghan's eyes widened. "Should I go to your office?"

Jack nodded. "Yes," he agreed. "Wait for me. This shouldn't take long."

When Jack returned to his office, his face was shell-shocked. "You won't believe what's happened," he whispered to Meghan.

"What's going on?" Meghan asked.

Jack took a long, deep breath. "Well, he didn't quite confess to murder," Jack informed Meghan as she leaned forward in her chair. "He told me that he and Roger had been sharing a bottle of vodka together on the night Roger died. They drank too much, and when Alan regained consciousness, he was lying in front of the toy store downtown. Roger was gone."

Meghan raised an eyebrow. "I don't understand," she murmured.

"There's more," Jack said. "Alan confessed that he and Roger were close friends. They had a falling out awhile back, but they were buddies. They told each other everything."

Meghan shook her head. "I don't understand."

Jack closed his eyes. "I think Alan knows more than he is letting on," he told Meghan. "It just doesn't make sense that these two old pals could spend the evening together, and then, Roger ended up dead. Alan has too much to lose in this case. I'm ordering him thrown back in jail, and I'm going to find out just how he killed Roger. Maybe he worked with Christian Evans, or maybe he worked alone, but either way, I have a feeling that he had something to do with it."

16

"MAMA? MAMA, YOU FORGOT YOUR SWEATER at the bakery. I came by to return it, like you asked me to."

Meghan stood outside of her parents' hotel room hoping they were available. She had been just about to close her eyes for a quick nap when her phone had rung; Rebecca insisted that she come to the hotel to return the sweater immediately, and Meghan had dutifully agreed. Now, as she stood in the hallway, she wished she had let her phone go to voicemail and taken her nap.

"Henry, I want to move here full-time," she heard her mother shout through the thick, oak door. "It isn't fair that I can't make the decision myself, and I think you are being a bully about this!"

Meghan heard the anger in her mother's voice, and she pressed her ear against the door. "Moving to Sandy Bay full-time is impossible, Rebecca," Henry announced. "I have business to attend to in Texas! You have your groups and social activities. Why would you want to give all of that up for this dinky little town?"

Meghan heard her mother sniffle. "I miss our Meghan," Rebecca cried. "She's been away for so long. We are practically strangers! She doesn't understand my sense of humor, or style, and I don't understand hers. I want to change that, Henry."

"Then why don't we stick with the original plan and buy a second home here?" Henry asked.

"It isn't enough," Rebecca pleaded. "I can tell that Meghan is in love with Jack, and before we know it, she will be getting married and having babies. I want some time to get to know my daughter as an adult, and I want that time before she is consumed with being a wife and a mother. I don't think that is too much to ask."

There was a long pause, and Meghan decided to let herself into the hotel room. She opened the door, and her parents stared at her. "Meghan," Rebecca exclaimed. "What are you doing here?"

Meghan held the mint green designer sweater up for her mother to see. "You asked me to bring this to you, remember?"

Rebecca nodded and smiled through her tears. "Of course, dear. I sure hope you didn't hear your Daddy and I quarreling in here. It's rude to let others hear your private matters, you know."

Henry nodded. "Your mother and I were just discussing the holiday," he lied to his daughter as Meghan politely nodded.

"Yes," Rebecca confirmed. "The holiday. Anyway, my phone is ringing; let me take this, and Henry? Can you offer Meghan some refreshments?"

Henry ushered Meghan further into the hotel suite. It was a magnificent set of rooms complete with an opulent master bedroom, a spare bedroom, three bathrooms, an in-suite study, and a personal butler to meet guests' every need. "This is a nice place, Daddy," Meghan said in awe as she examined the art on the wall. "This is nicer than my apartment."

"You know how your mother likes nice things," Henry told his daughter as he gestured at a leather armchair. "Sit down, Meghan. It's nearly happy hour. What can I make you to drink?"

Meghan thought for a moment. "A Tom Collins?"

"Coming right up," Henry informed her, walking to the yellow telephone on the wall and giving it a ring. "Hello? This is Henry Truman, and I would like to order a Tom Collins, a gin on the rocks, and a whiskey sour. Yes, we would also like some appetizers. Let's get an order of the spinach dip, the crab legs, eighteen oysters--no, make that twenty-four, and a spread of cheese and pate. Yes, charge it to the room. Thank you."

Meghan smiled. "You have quite the appetite, Daddy," she said as Henry settled in the chair next to hers.

Henry shrugged. "Your mother likes to have options," he explained. "And frankly, I am worn out from arguing with her. I need some food in my belly if I'm going to go around with her about it again."

"About what, Daddy?" Meghan pried.

Henry gave his daughter a knowing look. "I'm sure you heard us from the hallway," he stated. "Your mother wants to move here permanently, and much as I would love to be near you full time, my dear, it just won't work for our businesses. This is one of your mother's flights of fancy, and she just needs to accept that we are not moving here."

Suddenly, Rebecca burst into the sitting room, a joyful look on her face. "That was Kayley Kane on the phone," she exclaimed. "She has a new property that has *everything* I want, Henry! Everything. She assures me that it will meet all of my needs, and that it will be to my liking."

Henry shifted in his chair. "Rebecca, we just spoke about this," he told his wife. "Why don't you sit down? It's almost happy hour, and I've ordered snacks and drinks for all of us. I ordered you a whiskey sour, just the way you like it. Sit down, my dear, and let's just enjoy this time together. I don't want to spend another minute of our visit with Meghan fighting about properties or second homes."

Rebecca glared at her husband. "Henry, this is important to me," she hissed. "I want to see this property, and I want you to go with me. You are my husband, and I can't finalize anything without you. Come with me, fall in love with the place, and let's pursue it together. Please?"

Meghan stifled a giggle as her mother pouted dramatically, extending her bottom lip out and making sad eyes at Henry.

"Fine," Henry said. "Fine. But I hope you remember this in two weeks when we vacation in Greece. You will inevitably do this same song and dance and beg for a home there, and my answer will be----"

"Your answer will be whatever makes me happy," Rebecca informed her husband as she winked at him. "Meghan, this is a great lesson for you for someday: happy wife, happy life. Isn't that right, Henry, my love?"

The Trumans bundled up and walked the two blocks to Kayley's office. As Henry held the door for his wife and daughter, Lewis Templeton, the manager of the fine hotel where they were staying, marched outside with a grin on his face. He stopped to greet the Trumans, and Meghan was surprised with how familiar Lewis was with her parents; he kissed Rebecca on both cheeks and gave Henry a firm handshake.

"The Trumans," Lewis gushed. "Such lovely people. It's been such a delight hosting you in my hotel."

Rebecca blushed. Lewis was very handsome, and Meghan could see her mother's cheeks burning as she reveled in Lewis' compliments.

"You are a doll," Rebecca told Lewis. "You truly know good service, unlike other businesses around here. We went into that department store, and they had next to nothing on their racks. Unacceptable, yes?"

"Oh, yes," Lewis cooed as he dusted lint from his perfectly-tailored trousers. "To be honest, I am happy they might be going out of business."

"Oh?" Meghan asked. "Why is that?"

Lewis shrugged. "I feel torn regarding that department store's dealings with the homeless. On one hand, I think it's amazing that they gave away so much money to help someone get back on their feet. I do, however, think that we have a homeless *problem* here in Sandy Bay. The economic impact of the homeless population is undeniable; when they loiter, businesses typically see a decrease in their revenue, and as someone invested in this town's prosperity, I find it alarming that we encourage them through the department store contest."

Meghan raised an eyebrow at Lewis who stared into her dark eyes. He adjusted his popped collar and cleared his throat. "Look," he said to Meghan. "I *love* this town, just like you, Meghan, and I want it to grow. I have brought in so much business with the hotel, and I want to attract the right crowds. Like your parents. Rebecca and Henry are our ideal clients, and I want to see more fine people exploring what our sleepy little town has to offer. Sandy Bay is so beautiful, and with its proximity to the sea, well, I think we should be seeing more tourism than we are."

Meghan bit her lip. "I don't get it," she said to Lewis. "What does that have to do with our homeless population?"

Lewis sighed. "We have such a large homeless population," he said. "And "I think they drive away the right kind of people. Your mother told me that the group of homeless people outside of Luciano's was disturbing to her, and I can only imagine it would be disturbing to others."

"But there are homeless people everywhere," Meghan countered.

"Not so," Lewis argued. "Plenty of finer communities have rules that make it impossible for them to simply camp out in the towns. It's time we adopted those rules. I just met with Kayley about purchasing that lot next to Luciano's for a boutique inn, but I told her that if we can't eradicate the problem outside of Luciano's, I will have to pass on the property."

Meghan's eyes widened. "You mean eradicate the homeless?"

Lewis nodded. "Precisely. They simply must go if this town is going to thrive, Meghan, and I'm not going to let a gang of hooligans prevent my boutique inn from being the next best business in Sandy Bay. Thankfully, she has another perfect little bungalow ready for me to buy that isn't teeming with scoundrels. Anyway, I have to run; I'm due for some shopping and tea soon, and I'm already late. Toodles, Trumans!"

Meghan's heart pounded as her parents led her into Kayley's office. "Lewis seemed awfully eager to do away with the homeless people. Could he have anything to do with…"

"Trumans!" Kayley screeched as they walked into her office, interrupting Meghan's train of thought. "What a pleasure. Sit down, all of you."

"Nice to see you again, Ms. Kane," Rebecca said politely. "Tell me what you called us in for. We want all of the details."

Kayley glowed. "It's been such a great day," she chirped. "Lewis wanted to buy the property next to Luciano's, but another buyer came through last minute, so I was able to make quite the commission. Now, I have found the perfect property for you."

Meghan gasped. "So does the new owner care about the homeless people out front? Isn't that what Lewis was concerned about?"

Kayley winked. "I will take care of that little issue, no problem. Besides, it was the Luciano family who purchased the lot. They decided to get it and expand their business! Now, Trumans, let's get down to business. I have the ideal location for you. This property is on the coast, just outside of town. The main house has ten bedrooms, a workout facility, and an infinity pool on the second-story terrace. There is also a guest house with its own bedroom, bathroom, and kitchen, a pool house, and a private dock."

Henry grinned. "Private dock, huh? Okay, Rebecca, Ms. Kane has my attention now."

Kayley beamed. "With its marble fireplaces, original wood floors, and elegant interior, this property is one of the hottest on the entire west coast right now. There's even a little building on the property that could be turned into a shop for you to run in your spare time, Mrs. Truman."

Rebecca's eyes shined. "I think it sounds marvelous," she breathed as Kayley's face lit up like a star on a Christmas tree. "Kayley, I think you need to tell me every little detail."

Meghan raised her eyebrows, still thinking about their encounter with Lewis earlier. She was dismayed by his attitude toward the homeless, and his comment about eradicating them had startled her. "Kayley?"

Kayley looked up from the photographs of the beach property. "Yes, Meghan?"

Meghan took a deep breath. "Kayley, can you tell me more about the property next to Luciano's? I'm just confused as to why they would choose to expand at this kind of a time. What is Roberto thinking?"

Kayley shrugged. "It isn't my business," she said. "But to be honest, Roberto wasn't really the one driving the purchase…"

"Maria wants to expand?" Meghan asked. "His wife?"

Kayley shook her head. "No, it was Angela. She came in here with a business plan and some ideas, and after she and Lewis went around and around on bids, it appeared that Angela's offer was the best. It works out well for all involved, as I was able to sell another property to Lewis at a great price."

Suddenly, there was a knock on the door of Kayley's office. The Trumans' heads turned, and everyone smiled as Angela Luciano walked into the room.

"Speak of the devil," Henry said as he rose to his feet and shook Angela's hand. "Sounds like congratulations are in order, little lady. Ms. Kane here just told us that you purchased the lot next to your father's business and are hoping to expand."

Angela grinned. "Yes," she confirmed. "My father is letting me handle the expansion deal; we are going to put in a little Italian dessert alcove that connects to our restaurant. It will feature some of Italy's finest sweet treats, and I could not be more excited to handle this responsibility. I am honored my father and mother trust me so!"

Rebecca kissed Angela on both cheeks. "How lovely for you," she cooed. "We will certainly have to try your new place when it opens."

Angela nodded, her face bright with excitement. "That would be fantasticio," she declared. "We love having Jack and Meghan in for dinner, and we have certainly loved getting to know Meghan's lovely family."

Kayley interjected. "Speaking of Meghan's lovely family, I was just in a meeting with them to discuss a new property," Kayley matter-of-factly told Angela.

"Was I expecting you, Angela?"

"Oh, no," Angela told Kayley. "My father wanted me to stop by and see if you had the papers drawn up yet, and I was in the neighborhood and wanted to check."

Kayley shook her head. "No, they will be ready tomorrow," she told Angela. "But let me finish my meeting with the Trumans, and I'll be right with you."

"You found a property? Angela asked Rebecca. "How exciting. I suppose congratulations are in order for you as well. Sandy Bay is a world class town, and I am so happy to see it blossom."

Rebecca smiled. "We haven't decided yet," she told Angela as she glanced at her husband. "But I think we will make it work."

"That's wonderful," Angela exclaimed. "What a wonderful day for Sandy Bay to have the Trumans being part of our community."

At that moment, Meghan was hit with the realization that she was supposed to meet Jack for a movie at six. She glanced at her watch and realized it was six-fifteen. She frantically pulled out her cell phone and dialed Jack's number.

"Meghan, what are you doing?" Rebecca asked her daughter. "We're having a conversation with Angela and Kayley. Put your phone down right now."

"Sorry, Mama," she apologized. "I can't. I didn't

expect to be at your hotel today, and I completely forgot about my plans to meet Jack for a movie. I need to call him quickly. Excuse me."

Meghan stepped out of Kayley's office. As she closed the door, Jack picked up the phone call.

"Meghan? Where are you? Are you okay?"

She felt a knot in her stomach as she heard the concern in Jack's voice. "I'm fine," she told him. "Totally fine. I ended up running over to my parents' hotel room, and they coerced me into visiting Kayley Kane's office."

"What?" Jack asked in confusion.

"Kayley is looking for properties for my parents, remember? She found something Mama is interested in, and Mama dragged us all here tonight."

Jack sighed. "Well, I'm glad you are fine. I was worried about you."

"So sorry, Jack," she said. "I got caught here talking with my parents, Kayley, and Angela."

"Angela? Angela Luciano?"

"Yes, Angela Luciano," Meghan said. "What other Angelas do we know?"

"What is she doing at Kayley's office with you and your family?"

"I guess she purchased that lot next to her family business," she told him. "She's going to turn it into an Italian dessert place and attach it to her restaurant. Obviously, I don't love having her as competition; Angela is basically perfect in every regard. Like today, for example, I show up to this office in my sweats, and Angela is wearing this gorgeous red poncho that brings out her eyes. I feel like some sort of unsightly potato, haha. I am, however, excited to try some of her authentic Italian treats. Maybe she and I can collaborate on something in the future."

Jack took a long breath. "Meghan? Is Angela sitting next to you right now?"

"No," she replied.

"Where is she?"

"She's in Kayley's office chatting with my folks. I stepped out to give you a call."

The phone went dead, and Meghan tried to redial Jack's number. It went straight to his voicemail, and Meghan pursed her lips. She walked back into the office and resumed her place in the chair beside her parents.

"How is Jack? Was he fussy that you forgot about your plans? Really, Meghan, I didn't raise you like this; you should have a proper day planner and write down your engagements so that you don't miss anything."

Meghan gritted her teeth as her mother chided her.

"Jack is fine," she told Rebecca. "He didn't seem mad.

"I would have been downright annoyed," Henry announced as Rebecca nodded. "It's not nice to miss dates."

Meghan pasted a smile on her lips. "Well, he said it is fine," she reiterated. "The only weird part of our conversation was the end. He hung up the phone abruptly, or his phone died. It was weird. I tried dialing it back, and I can't get through to him."

"Maybe missing your date wasn't as "okay" as you thought," Rebecca smirked.

The color drained from Angela's face. "I really should be going," she said as she rose to her feet and pushed in her chair. "Kayley, it was a pleasure, as always. Trumans, I hope to see you all before you leave. Ciao for now, to all of you."

"Stop right there."

Meghan gasped as Jack appeared in the doorway, a gun in his hand. Behind him were three other Sandy Bay police officers, all holding weapons of their own.

"Jack? What's going on here?" Meghan whimpered.

"That's a nice gun," Henry chuckled. "The boy will fit right in in Texas, won't he, Rebecca?"

Jack shook his head. "This is no time for jokes," he declared. "Angela Luciano, you are under arrest for the murder of Roger Williams!"

17

"WHAT?" ANGELA SPUTTERED as everyone stared at her. "What are you talking about, Jack?"

"It's *Detective Irvin* to you," he told Angela as he fastened a pair of handcuffs around her slim wrists. "Angela, we have hard evidence of your crimes. It's time you come with us to the station."

Angela squirmed as a female deputy helped her to her feet. "Get off of me," she cried. "I had nothing to do with Roger's death. I wouldn't kill a fly."

"You may not kill flies," Jack announced. "But you certainly made your mark on the homeless population here by killing five homeless people in the last two weeks, starting with Roger."

Meghan gasped. "Jack, this can't be true. Angela is a *devoted* volunteer for the homeless. She is a champion for their plight. You should see her at the food bank; she has such a passion for helping them."

Jack scoffed. "More like a passion for *murdering* them," he corrected his girlfriend. "We have proof that Angela Luciano killed several homeless people in cold blood."

"Jack, this is terribly frightening," Rebecca whimpered. "Put those guns down."

"Seriously," Kayley snapped. "You're gonna break something in my office. Either get Angela out of here, or you get out of here, Jack."

Jack motioned to the female deputy to take Angela away, but Henry stepped between her and Angela. "Now, Jack," Henry argued. "This little lady and her family have been nothing but good to my family. It would be a shame to further distress her. Look how scared she is."

"Yes," Angela sobbed. "I am so scared. Please, Jack, let me go."

"It's Detective Irvin," Jack replied coldly. "And Henry? I need you to sit down; I'm doing my job here, and you are in the way. Have a seat."

Henry frowned, but obeyed Jack's order. Jack turned to stare at Angela.

"Angela, I have no choice here; there is evidence that you are to blame for these deaths, and I am under orders to take you in."

The female officer led Angela out of the office, and Jack nodded at Kayley and the Trumans. "I apologize that you had to see that," he said as he put his hands in his pockets.

Meghan frowned. "What is the evidence, Jack?" she asked. "Everyone in town knows that Christian Evans killed Roger. What about Lewis from the hotel? Maybe he had something to do with it. I talked to him today, and he said some nasty things about the homeless people."

Jack pursed his lips. "Saying nasty things and *doing* nasty things are two different stories," he explained to his girlfriend. "We have investigated Christian's misdeeds, and he is guilty of a lot, but he has not killed anyone. Lewis is just full of hot air, Meghan. It's Angela who killed Roger, along with several others, and it's Angela who is on her way to jail."

Rebecca frowned. "It just seems scandalous to take a pretty young lady like Angela off to jail," she admonished.

Jack shook his head. We have *proof.* One of the busboys at Luciano's took his dog into the vet; he thought the dog had been poisoned by a mean neighbor, and he filed a complaint with the police."

Henry wrinkled his nose. "What does a sick dog have to do with any of this?"

"A lot, actually," Jack continued. "We looked into the complaint, and after speaking with the busboy, we learned that Angela had stayed late at the restaurant the night the dog became ill. We went through the sick dog's stool, and after testing, it was determined that the only thing in his stomach was food from Luciano's. Just for curiosity's sake, I decided to review the security footage from outside of Luciano's that night. Well, who was outside at 1am?"

Henry shook his head. "I don't understand this, Jack."

Jack shrugged. "Angela was outside, and the footage caught her feeding sandwiches to the little dog right before she took a bag of sandwiches to the homeless fellows outside. We have footage that shows her giving them food. Most of them were asleep, and the fellow who died, Roger, gobbled up all of the sandwiches by himself."

Meghan's eyes widened. "So Angela gave *poisoned* food to the dog and the homeless guys?"

"Exactly." Jack confirmed.

"Are you sure about this, Jack?"

Jack smiled. "I wasn't sure until ten minutes ago when Meghan and I spoke," he said. "The security footage was grainy enough that we couldn't quite make out the face of the killer, but we could see them in a red poncho. Well, remember what Angela was wearing?"

Meghan gasped. "She was wearing her red poncho," she whispered. "The same one Jack had described from the film."

Jack nodded. "It's terrible," he admitted. "But think about it: she has a clear motive. Angela wanted to get rid of the homeless population one by one so that she could continue to grow her business. It makes sense. I can't believe I didn't think of it sooner."

Rebecca slumped back in her chair. "Well, that was a shock," she uttered as she dramatically fanned her face. "I cannot believe that Angela was the killer. What a terrible crime from such a lovely girl."

Henry shook his head. "That's what happens when ambition turns to poison," he declared. He pointed a finger at Meghan. "Don't you ever let your business stand in the way of you doing the right thing and treating people well. Business and ambition can turn even the purest hearts to stone, and that's what happened to Angela Luciano."

"Oh, Daddy," Meghan said as she reached to hug her father. "I love my work, and I love serving the people of Sandy Bay, but my business is just a business to me. I'm passionate about my shop, but I would never, ever harm anyone in pursuit of my own success."

"Good girl," Henry said as he hugged his daughter. "And Ms. Kane, I hope you follow the same principles. I know you are a successful gal, but I hope tonight's events teach you a good lesson, too."

Kayley stared at Mr. Truman. She yawned, looking bored, and examined her nails.

"Kayley?" Mr. Truman pressed.

Kayley sighed. "I'll never let my business or ambitions stand in the way of someone else's health or well-being," she said robotically as Henry and Rebecca nodded and smiled. "But that doesn't mean I won't do everything in my power to get to the top every other way."

Meghan laughed. "We know, Kayley," she said. "We know."

That night, Meghan shared a quiet dinner with her parents back at the hotel. The news of Angela's arrest was all over Sandy Bay, and Meghan wanted a reprieve from the heinous story of the beautiful, remorseless killer. She ordered a variety of tacos and three types of queso from her favorite street taco vendor and asked her father to order margaritas from the hotel bar.

"That's a lot of fattening food," Rebecca said as Meghan walked in with the bags of tacos.

"Daddy said you like options, so I brought options," Meghan replied. "Besides, we had a long night, and I need some good food to help me relax. Come on, Mama, try the pork tacos. Or try the fish tacos. I think you will love the lime sauce."

Rebecca sighed, but took a seat next to Meghan on the velvet couch. She unwrapped a chicken taco and took a bite. "This is quite good," she admitted. "Thank you for bringing dinner to us."

"No problem," Meghan said. "It's the least I could do. I know you are upset now that the beach house deal is off."

Rebecca shrugged. "Given tonight's events, your father and I just don't feel as though it's the right time or place to make such an investment," she told her daughter. "We do want to see you more, Meghan, and we are going to make every effort to be bigger parts of your life. We love you, and we miss you, and we want to watch you grow into the wonderful woman you are becoming."

Meghan's eyes filled with tears at her mother's compliments. Rebecca was certainly hard to please, and Meghan was thrilled that her mother acknowledged her hard work and growth. "Thank you, Mama," Meghan whispered as she returned her taco to its plate and hugged her mother.

"Careful, this dress is Dior," Rebecca warned Meghan as she leaned away.

"Your mother and I have talked, and we want you and Jack to visit us in Texas in the New Year," Henry announced as he strode into the sitting area carrying a tray of margaritas. "Jack is a good man, and he will take care of you. I trust him, and I think we need to get to know him better."

Meghan smiled. "I would like that, Daddy," she told him.

"Perfect," he said. "We'll purchase some tickets for you two for Christmas. How does first-class sound? That will be our gift to the pair of you, a trip to Texas on us."

"That sounds amazing," Meghan squealed, jumping up to hug her father. "What a sweet gift. Thank you both!"

18

ONE WEEK LATER, on Christmas Eve, Meghan and Jack were hosting the Trumans for a farewell brunch at Truly Sweet. Meghan had gone above and beyond to cook a feast her parents would love; she had made gourmet omelettes, chicken sausage, fresh caramel strudel, and a hot plate of turkey bacon. Jack had helped set the table with Meghan's nicest dishes, and as they ate, Meghan's parents clucked over the meal she had prepared.

Meghan was quite proud of herself. Dressed in her favorite maroon dress, her dark hair tumbled down her back, and from the look on Jack's face when she answered the door, she knew she looked beautiful. Her mother had even complimented her on the outfit, and as she served brunch to her parents, Meghan felt as though she were finally being treated as the adult business owner she was.

"It's perfect, Meghan," Henry told his daughter as he stuffed a third piece of bacon in his mouth.

"Truly sweet, Sugar," Rebecca agreed. "You are quite the hostess. I am so impressed by the little soiree you have thrown together for us. You have been quite the hostess this holiday season!"

Meghan smiled. Her mother was referring to the event she had held at the bakery the previous day. Given the events of the season, Meghan's heart hurt for the homeless population in Sandy Bay. She, Pamela, Trudy, and Rebecca had spent an entire day preparing an abundance of treats, and Meghan had hosted a holiday celebration for the homeless folks in town. She had hired a group of carolers to sing festive songs, made pretty decorations, and even organized a variety of games and activities for her guests. The event had made the local news, and Meghan was pleased to learn that the publicity had drawn attention to the homeless population, and donations had been flooding in for the food bank.

"This is a great thing you're doing for the folks who are down on their luck," Jack had told Meghan at the event. "You are a truly sweet woman, Meghan."

"It's my pleasure to do it for them," Meghan told her boyfriend. "These people have so little and we have so much. Why not take time to give back? This is the way businesses should be run--to not only make profits, but to give back to the community."

The event drew over ninety people into the bakery, and Meghan was pleased that every last treat had been taken by the end of the night. As she showered and prepared for bed after she had bid the last guest farewell, she was certain that she had done the right thing by opening her business to those in need. She loved serving others, and she made a vow to keep the homeless in mind as she moved forward.

Now, on Christmas Eve, Meghan was glowing as she basked in the attention of her parents.
Meghan leaned back in her chair, pleased by their compliments. "Thank you both," she told them. "And thank you for visiting. I am so sad that you are leaving today, and I am so disappointed that you won't be buying a second home here."

Rebecca shrugged. "It was going to be an impulse buy," she admitted. "Now that I know that you are safe here with Jack, I don't think we need to buy another home. I *do*, however, think that we need to invest in a better airline credit card, don't you, Henry? We will be missing our girl terribly, and I want to visit Sandy Bay more than once a year! We can't wait for you two to visit Texas, but I don't want to wait until the summer to see you again. I plan to visit next month, and Henry, I hope you will help me make the arrangements."

Henry nodded. "Yes, we will certainly do that," he told his wife. "I'm just glad to know that the homeless population here is not dangerous. It was a shock to hear that Angela killed that man, but the entire situation has just touched my heart. Meghan, your mother and I have agreed to donate ten thousand dollars to the food bank this Christmas, and we want you to deliver the check to the organization."

Meghan's eyes filled with tears. "Thank you, Daddy," she murmured as she rose from her chair and moved to hug her father. "Thank you, Mama. This means so much to me."

Henry nodded. "We were just so impressed with your kindness," he told his daughter. "You gave away so many of your treats to the homeless, not to mention your attention and time. That spirit of philanthropy inspired me, Meghan, and I plan to incorporate that into my own business ventures. You have certainly made us proud."

Jack also rose to his feet and gently tapped Henry on the shoulder. "Henry? Can we talk privately for a moment?"

Henry nodded and followed Jack into the kitchen. "Henry," Jack began as he shifted nervously. "I love your daughter. I would do anything for her. She is an amazing woman, and I have something I need to ask you."

Henry smiled. "I think I know where this is going. What do you need to ask me, Jack?"

Jack grinned. "I want you to know that I am saving for a ring for Meghan. With your blessing, I want to ask her to marry me in the year to come. I will have enough money put away to buy a ring in a few months, and by next Christmas, I would like for Meghan to be my wife."

Henry beamed. He pulled Jack into a tight hug. "You have my blessing, sport," he told Jack. "Now, just make sure you run that ring by Rebecca before you buy it; Meghan's mother has an affinity for nice things, and surely she'll want you to have her opinion. Meghan is easy to please; surely she will love whatever you find for her, but you know my wife..."

Jack laughed. "I'm sure that will be an interesting conversation when the time comes. Anyway, thank you for your support, Henry. It truly means the world. I cannot wait to ask Meghan to marry me. Now, I just need to keep saving for the ring, and I need to plan the proposal."

Henry shook Jack's hand. "My pleasure, son. I'm happy for the pair of you. Meghan sparkles when she is with you, and I see from the look in your eyes right now that you are excited for this next step in your life. I remember feeling this way the night I met Rebecca. I was at a party, and I took a bite of this amazing coconut tart. It was topped with roasted pineapple, and it was to die for. Anyway, I asked to meet the cook, and sure enough, Rebecca had made the treat."

Jack smiled. "That's a great story."

Henry nodded. "It gets better. Rebecca's tarts brought us together, and on the night we were engaged, little did I know that she had spent all morning making my favorite tarts for me. Everytime I think about those tarts, and the woman behind them, I get that look in my eye...the same one you have now."

Jack chuckled. "I'm lucky to have found a Truman woman."

Henry winked. "Yes, you are, Jack Irvin. Hmmm. Meghan Irvin. That sounds nice I think. Now! Let's get back to brunch. I am going to pour some champagne into our orange juices...I believe we have

Henry winked. "Yes, you are, Jack Irvin. Hmmm. Meghan Irvin. That sounds nice I think. Now! Let's get back to brunch. I am going to pour some champagne into our orange juices...I believe we have something to celebrate, even if my little girl doesn't know it yet."

Jack followed Henry back into the dining room and grinned as Henry poured the bubbly into everyone's glass.

"Daddy?" Meghan asked. "What is this for? You two are traveling today! Are you sure you want to dive into the champagne?"

Henry winked at his daughter, and then shot a look at Jack. Jack blushed, and Henry laughed. "I'm sure, Meghan," Henry said. "Absolutely sure."

"Henry, you know what champagne does to my stomach," Rebecca protested. Henry reached over and whispered Jack's news into Rebecca's ear, and she squealed.

"What, Mama?" Meghan asked. "What is this fuss about?"

Rebecca quickly regained her composure. "Oh, it's nothing, dear," she told her daughter. "Nothing. Let's just have a nice little breakfast drink and a toast."

"A toast," Henry announced. "To our little girl and her big heart, her big business, her big dreams, and her *big, bright* future. I believe Meghan will have a lot of joy in the year ahead. Merry Christmas to you, my girl, and happy holidays to all of you. Cheers!"

"Cheers!" everyone called out.

As everyone lifted their glasses, Meghan felt a happy tear trail from her eyes. She looked at her father, who was merrily raising a glass in her honor, and to her mother, whose time in Sandy Bay had been precious to her. Meghan lastly looked at Jack, her handsome boyfriend. She loved Jack with all of her heart, and as she sat next to him on Christmas Eve, she hoped that she would spend every Christmas with Jack.

"Cheers," Meghan exclaimed as she lifted her own glass. "Cheers to the sweetest days ahead."

The End

Jingle Bells and Deadly Smells

Afterword

Thank you for reading Jingle Bells and Deadly Smells! I really hope you enjoyed reading it as much as I had writing it!

If you have a minute, please consider leaving a review on Amazon.

Many thanks in advance for your support!

About King Cake and Grave Mistakes

Released: January, 2019
Series: Book 11 – Sandy Bay Cozy Mystery Series
Standalone: Yes
Cliff-hanger: No

A spate of muggings. A murdered victim. Can a small town bakery owner solve the case before the killer ending?

Meghan Truman has cornered the desserts market in the Pacific Northwest. With her twin poodles by her side, the once-upon-a-time newbie in town is set to grow her mini empire. But Meghan has a real-life murder mystery on her hands when a pampering party for a famous painter ends with the demise of a guest.

How could a girly night of fun and laughter with some tasty nibbles end on such a sour note?

As Meghan continues her investigation, she discovers one common denominator links all the suspects on her list: their relationship to the famous painter...plus their consumption of her king cake!

With her boyfriend, handsome detective Jack Irvin out of town, will Meghan discover the mistakes the killer made to link them to the murder?

KING CAKE AND GRAVE MISTAKES
CHAPTER 1 SNEAK PEEK

IT WAS A DULL, DARK EVENING in January, and twenty-seven year old Meghan Truman was fighting a serious case of the winter blues. Nearly three weeks into the New Year, the novelty of the holiday season had worn off, and Meghan's life in Sandy Bay, a small town in the Pacific Northwest, felt drab and dreary. Meghan's professional life was booming; as the sole owner of Truly Sweet, a quaint bakery that had gained enormous popularity over the last few months, Meghan could hardly keep up with the incoming requests for treats, and the new sets of corporate orders seeming to pour in each day.

"I need to do something to perk myself up," Meghan thought to herself as she scrubbed the front counter of the bakery. "I've felt down in the dumps for the last few days. I wish I could call Jack."

Meghan's heart sank at the thought of her tall, handsome boyfriend, Jack Irvin. With his blonde hair and bright blue eyes, Meghan swooned every time she looked at him. Jack was a detective, and for the next two weeks, he was out of town in New Orleans for a special training. Meghan had anticipated his time away would feel fast; her schedule was so busy, and she hardly had time for herself. Yet, while Jack had been gone for only two days, it had felt like two years.

Meghan glanced out at the gloomy night. The thick snow covering the town had melted into a gray mess, and the bitter winter sea gusts cut through Meghan's coat every time she stepped outside. She longed for the mild winters of Los Angeles, the city she had lived in before moving to Sandy Bay, and even more, she desperately ached for the hot, humid winters of Texas, the state where she had grown up.

Suddenly, Meghan looked over at the bulletin board next to the rack of aprons and was struck with inspiration. Pinned to the board was a pamphlet from the salon in town, owned by her good friend, Jackie. Meghan remembered that Jackie was hosting late-night salon hours this week as a January special, and she grinned. She had sent her employees home hours ago, and after finishing her preparations for the next day, Meghan knew it was time to leave the bakery for the night. She looked down at her hands. Meghan's palms were calloused from hours of kneading dough, her fingers had small abrasions from dicing fruit, and her cuticles were wild and overgrown. "I know what I'm going to do," Meghan exclaimed as she examined her rough hands. "I'm going to get a manicure at Jackie's. I'll be right in time to catch her late night hours, and my hands could use some pampering. Everyone is gone for the night, my work is finished, and I think it's time to take care of myself.

Twenty minutes later, Meghan skipped into the Sandy Bay salon owned by her good friend, Jackie. Meghan hadn't dressed up and had hastily thrown her long, dark hair into a messy bun, unaware of how upscale Jackie's clientele would be. It wasn't until she looked down at the floor in the waiting area and saw designer bag after designer bag perched next to their glamorous owners.

"Maybe I should have showered before leaving the bakery," Meghan thought as she peered at the other guests lounging in the waiting area. "That woman is dripping in jewelry, and that man over there has shoes that must have cost him a fortune. I hope I don't embarrass Jackie with my messy hair and sweatpants; it looks like the people in here are way fancier than I expected."

Meghan fidgeted in her seat as she surveyed the waiting area. The spacious room was lit by three sparkling chandeliers, and the white tile floors were covered with Persian rugs. A fountain in the corner held several large, exotic-looking fish, and the receptionist's desk was made from what appeared to be crystal.

"Jackie never mentioned how nice this place has gotten," Meghan grumbled as a lithe, blonde woman glided into the salon.

"Meghan!"

Meghan smiled weakly as Jackie appeared. "Thanks for squeezing me in, Jackie," Meghan told her friend as Jackie kissed her on both cheeks. "The salon looks amazing, Jackie. When did it become so classy?"

Jackie shrugged. "My internet-based business coach, Donna, suggested that I spruce things up a little," she explained to Meghan. "Donna thinks I should create an atmosphere for the clients I want, and the clients I want have a lot of money," she whispered to Meghan. "During the holidays, I had some spare time, and I decided to do a little shopping to make this place shine."

Meghan's eyes widened. "It looks like you did more than a little shopping," she laughed nervously as Jackie led her back to the manicure room. "This place looks so nice. I don't think I'm dressed well enough to even breathe the air here, Jackie."

Jackie shook her head. "Enough of that kind of talk, Meghan," she chided. "You are a friend of mine, and you belong here. Come sit! I have just enough time to give you a fabulous new color and nail shape before my next appointment arrives. Oh, Meghan, I am so glad you called. I've been dying to get my hands on your nails."

"This is just what I needed," Meghan admitted as she settled into the plush red chair in front of the manicure station.

"Good," Jackie agreed as she glanced down at her rose gold watch. "Yikes. Meghan, I have another client scheduled for eyelash extensions that I completely forgot about. I'm going to have my two assistants start taking care of you. Dolly? Polly?"

Two identical brunette girls appeared by Jackie's side. They looked young--Meghan guessed they were in their early twenties--and Meghan could not tell them apart.

"Meghan, these are my assistants, Dolly and Polly. They are new to the salon, but I hope they give you the best experience. I know they will, right girls?"

The two girls nodded, and Meghan smiled warmly at them. "It's fine,' she told Jackie. "We'll be fine."

Jackie scurried off, and Dolly lifted Meghan's left hand into a small silver bowl while Polly moved Meghan's right hand into a matching silver bowl. They worked in sync, both moving and breathing at the same pace. Meghan was mesmerized by their precision, and she stared as the twins pampered her.

"Meghan? You doing okay?"

Meghan's body jerked as she heard Jackie's voice. She realized she had been sleeping; she was so relaxed as the twins did her nails that she had drifted off to sleep.

"I'm good," she sleepily said to Jackie. "This is so cozy; the twins are doing a great job."

"What color did you pick?" Jackie asked.

Polly held up a bottle of the Josie Posie polish. "She selected this Josie Posie pink," Polly told Jackie.

"I think Jack will like it," Meghan gushed. "He always compliments me when I wear pink."

Jackie winked. "I think you're right. Ugh, Meghan, I have to run. I have to get over to the other manicure station. One of my clients is being a little...demanding...so I am going to go relieve my other assistant. I just wanted to check on you."

Meghan grinned. "Hey, I'm an easy client," she joked with her friend. "Just let the twins take care of me, and I will float on out of here."

Meghan smiled at the twins as Jackie flew away. "I really miss my boyfriend," she confided in them. "He's been gone a few days, and I'm a little lonely."

Before the twins could respond, Meghan heard a screech. "Seriously? You seriously think it is acceptable to leave my nails looking like that? This color is atrocious. It looks like a circus clown stuck his hands into a tomato patch. I can't believe this is the quality of the service here."

Meghan looked over her shoulder to see Jackie forcing herself to smile. "Rosie, my assistant simply didn't pair the color correctly. I am happy to give you a new color and comp it. My treat."

Meghan raised an eyebrow. Rosie, the woman who had screeched, looked glamorous. She had sharp features, with a pointed nose and bold jawline, and white blonde hair cut bluntly just above her collarbone. She was dressed in white leather pants, a black cashmere turtleneck, and matching white heeled boots.

"I don't have the time to wait for another color, Jackie," Rosie complained. "I'm meeting my boss for dinner in twenty minutes."

Meghan watched as Jackie bent down beside Rosie and began to work. "Just give me ten minutes, Rosie, and I'll have you out of here."

True to her word, ten minutes later, Rosie was beaming and kissing Jackie on the cheek as she rose from her chair and examined her nails. "Thank you, I owe you one," Rosie cooed as Jackie grinned.

"It's really no problem," Jackie assured Rosie as she escorted her to the waiting area. "I apologize my assistant did not deliver on the color you desired."

"Well, you fixed it so promptly that I have nearly forgotten all about it," Rosie said with a wink. "But really, I owe you one, Jackie. I'll see you next week for my appointment."

As Rosie sashayed out the door of the salon, Meghan gestured for Jackie to come over. Meghan's hands were deep in a dryer, and she was eager to hear about Jackie's customer. "Who was that?" Meghan asked. "Is she local? I've never seen her in town before."

Jackie rolled her eyes. "She's the personal assistant to someone important...I have to admit though, I've always tuned her out whenever she starts bragging about her job.

Meghan nodded. "Got it. She seemed like a real piece of work," she said.

Jackie laughed. "You have no idea."

Later that evening, after Jackie closed up the salon, she asked Meghan if she would run some errands with her. "We haven't gotten to catch up since New Year's," Jackie lamented. "Hop in my car and chat with me. I only have a few places to go, and it would be nice to have someone to talk with."

Meghan agreed, and she accompanied Jackie on her errands. They visited the grocery, the pharmacy, and the library, happily chatting as they made their purchases.

"Can I ask you a question?" Jackie asked as they headed toward the post office.

"Of course," Meghan replied.

Jackie took a deep breath. "How did you really get your business off of the ground, Meghan?"

Meghan cocked her head to the side. "What do you mean?"

Jackie bit her lip. "Well, things are on the up and up with the salon, but I want to really rock it. How did you do it with your bakery? Things were slow for you, and then they just took off."

Meghan shrugged. "It was the corporate orders," she admitted. "I love serving the people of Sandy Bay, but when I started catering for several of the big companies, I really saw the dollar pour in."

Jackie nodded. "I'm hoping some slam dunk client wanders in sooner than later," she sighed. "Someone rolling in the dough, you know?"

Jackie slammed on the brakes. "Hey!" she screamed, narrowly avoiding a pedestrian who had darted in front of the car. "Watch where you are going."

Meghan's heart was pounding. "What was she doing?"

Jackie glared as the female pedestrian scurried inside of the post office "People are so careless. She was probably on her phone, distracted."

Both women unbuckled their seatbelts, Meghan's heart still beating rapidly as Jackie turned off the car.

"Last stop," Jackie declared. "This will be a quick stop, I promise."

As Meghan and Jackie walked into the post office, Meghan gasped. "Jackie," she whispered. "Isn't that Rosie? From the salon?"

"Oh goodness," Jackie muttered. "It is. We have to say hi, even though I don't feel like dealing with her again."

"Darling Jackie!"

Meghan watched Jackie paste a smile on her face as

Rosie spotted Jackie.

"Hello, Rosie," Jackie said. "Good to see you."

Meghan noticed a woman in sunglasses behind Rosie. The woman had waist-length sandy hair, and wore a long pink coat. She was curvy, and her expensive outfit made her look womanly and beautiful. It was the same woman who had darted in front of Jackie's car only moments before.

"Jackie, Jackie's friend, this is the esteemed Mariah Cooper," Rosie said as the woman in sunglasses nodded at them. "She is an artist, and my dearest friend."

Meghan watched as Jackie's jaw dropped. "Mariah Cooper? The Mariah Cooper?"

Mariah Cooper pushed her sunglasses atop her head and nodded. "Yes, Mariah Cooper," she said coolly. "I believe you almost ran me over out there?"

"I...I….I'm so sorry," Jackie sputtered. "I didn't realize it was you."

Meghan saw the desperation in Jackie's face. Hoping to ease the tension, she smiled and reached out her hand. "Nice to meet you," she said. "I'm Jackie's friend, Meghan. Mariah, I hear you are a great painter and sculptor."

Mariah turned up her nose as Rosie shook her head. "She isn't just a great painter and sculptor," Rosie informed Meghan. "Her work is iconic. She is only twenty-seven years old, and her work is being featured at the Winter Olympics next year. She is internationally acclaimed."

Meghan playfully shrugged. "Does she ever speak for herself?"

Rosie's jaw dropped. "I don't think you understand," she said dismissively. "Mariah doesn't just talk to anyone. She is famous."

Jackie gently pushed Meghan behind her. "Meghan is just being silly," she said apologetically. "She is a jokester. Anyway, Rosie, Mariah, it was a pleasure. We must be going."

As Jackie and Meghan walked out of the post office, Jackie hissed at Meghan. "You could have jeopardized my business with Rosie with your sass."

Meghan bit her lip. "I was just trying to get them to get over themselves," she said. "I know that type, and they seemed so stuck up."

Jackie scowled. "That wasn't your place. You should just play it good next time, Meghan, if you know what's good for you. Mariah Cooper could be that slam dunk client I've been hoping for!"

You can order your copy of **King Cake and Grave Mistakes** at any good online retailer.

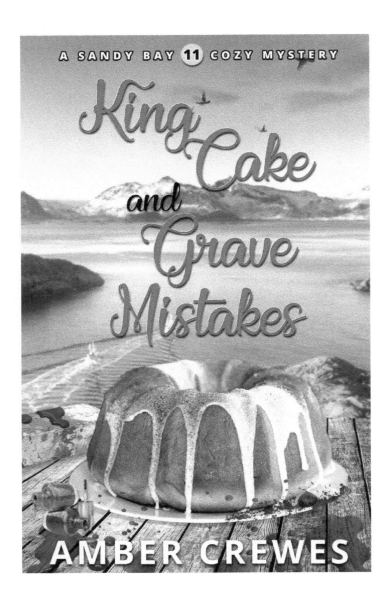

Amber Crewes

A SANDY BAY **11** COZY MYSTERY

King Cake and Grave Mistakes

AMBER CREWES

ALSO BY AMBER CREWES

The Sandy Bay Cozy Mystery Series

Apple Pie and Trouble

Brownies and Dark Shadows

Cookies and Buried Secrets

Donuts and Disaster

Éclairs and Lethal Layers

Finger Foods and Missing Legs

Gingerbread and Scary Endings

Hot Chocolate and Cold Bodies

Ice Cream and Guilty Pleasures

Jingle Bells and Deadly Smells

King Cake and Grave Mistakes

Lemon Tarts and Fiery Darts

Muffins and Coffins

Newsletter Signup

Want **FREE** COPIES OF FUTURE **AMBER CREWES** BOOKS, FIRST NOTIFICATION OF NEW RELEASES, CONTESTS AND GIVEAWAYS?

GO TO THE LINK BELOW TO SIGN UP TO THE NEWSLETTER!

www.AmberCrewes.com/cozylist

Jingle Bells and Deadly Smells

Amber Crewes

CPSIA information can be obtained
at www.ICGtesting.com
Printed in the USA
LVHW031949120121
676308LV00005B/732